"I hate it her[e]"

Rocco took anoth[er]

Noelle simply stared at him. "You... You hate it?"

"Yes. Everyone knows you, they talk to you constantly. It is saccharine to the point of being sickening, and I am not talking about the hot chocolate. The decorations are too bright, and it is too much. But you clearly love it."

"I do," she said.

"You love it, and you would do anything to preserve your life here, yes?"

"Yes."

Her heart was pounding. She didn't know where this was going.

"I have something to ask you."

"Okay."

He looked around the street, and the Christmas lights reflected in his dark eyes. Then he looked back at her, and they were nothing but coal black. "Noelle Holiday, I want you to be my wife."

Millie Adams has always loved books. She considers herself a mix of Anne Shirley (loquacious but charming and willing to break a slate over a boy's head if need be) and Charlotte Doyle (a lady at heart but with the spirit to become a mutineer should the occasion arise). Millie lives in a small house on the edge of the woods, which she finds allows her to escape in the way she loves best—in the pages of a book. She loves intense alpha heroes and the women who dare to go toe-to-toe with them (or break a slate over their heads).

Books by Millie Adams

Harlequin Presents

His Secretly Pregnant Cinderella
The Billionaire's Baby Negotiation
A Vow to Set the Virgin Free
The Forbidden Bride He Stole
Her Impossible Boss's Baby

The Kings of California

The Scandal Behind the Italian's Wedding
Stealing the Promised Princess
Crowning His Innocent Assistant
The Only King to Claim Her

From Destitute to Diamonds

The Billionaire's Accidental Legacy
The Christmas the Greek Claimed Her

The Diamond Club

Greek's Forbidden Temptation

Visit the Author Profile page
at Harlequin.com for more titles.

ITALIAN'S CHRISTMAS ACQUISITION

MILLIE ADAMS

Harlequin
PRESENTS

Harlequin® **PRESENTS**™

ISBN-13: 978-1-335-93924-1

Italian's Christmas Acquisition

 Harlequin Enterprises ULC
22 Adelaide St. West, 41st Floor
Toronto, Ontario M5H 4E3, Canada
www.Harlequin.com

Printed in Lithuania

Recycling programs for this product may not exist in your area.

MIX
Paper | Supporting responsible forestry
FSC® C021394

ITALIAN'S CHRISTMAS ACQUISITION

To Taylor Swift—for the music, the inspiration and the quality time spent being a fangirl with my daughter.

CHAPTER ONE

Christmas in Snowflake Falls, Wyoming, was Noelle Holiday's absolute favorite time of year. Not just because she was aptly named for the season—but being the daughter of two Christmas tree farm owners who also had a themed bed-and-breakfast might have contributed to it—but because it was just so...cheery.

The town was resplendent. There were lights strung on every available surface, the historic main street aglow with cheer. It was the calm before the storm for her, and like clockwork, she'd been craving her favorite Christmas drink this morning. So even though a trip to town hadn't been mandatory, it had felt vital.

The tree in the town square was vibrant, with large colored lights and brilliant rainbow ornaments. The tree had of course come from her farm. The one she selected to occupy the center of town was always her very best.

Even though it was early, the streets were bustling as people emerged from their hotels and homes to get caffeine.

Noelle was also on the hunt for caffeine. She dipped

into her favorite coffeehouse, a little brick building at the end of the lane, and stepped up to the counter.

"Can I have a gingerbread latte, please?"

"Is it opening day?" her friend Melody asked, smiling from her position behind the counter.

Sweet Melody really did have the best coffee in town, but the fact that it was owned by one of her best friends made it even better.

"Yes," Noelle said. "How did you know?"

"The antlers."

Noelle laughed. She had forgotten that she wasn't wearing a regular headband, rather one designed as part of her reindeer costume. Her brown sweater dress and brown fuzzy tights, along with her brown boots, completed the look. She shook her head, and the bells on the ends of the antler tines jingled. "At least I don't have my light-up nose on yet," she said. "You can't drink a latte easily with a lighted nose on."

"You'll probably attract a lot of attention, too," said Melody.

"I probably already am."

"True."

Her friend turned and began to make her drink, adding flavoring to a brightly colored cup, steaming milk and making a shot. Noelle knew that she was attracting attention, but she also didn't mind. He family had owned the Holiday House bed-and-breakfast and Christmas tree farm for generations. Her name was literally synonymous with the season. Anyway, it probably wasn't even that notable that she was wandering around dressed as a reindeer. If she wasn't a reindeer, then she was an elf, when the farm was open. And this being the day after Thanksgiving, that meant the season was well and truly in full swing.

Many other places in the US had a different kind of consumerism in full swing on days like today, but not Snowflake Falls. They didn't boast any chain stores, no massive Black Friday sales. Their little Main Street did come alive during the winter ski season. It had become an incredibly trendy place for people to stay, rivaling Jackson as the hotspot for Californians looking for snow. Some of the boutiques of late had become more chic, and there had been a few swathes of land bought with an eye toward making them into luxury resorts.

She tried not to think about that. She tried not to let that distract her.

Her mom was amping to sell the Christmas tree farm, and the B and B. Quite a few parcels of land around them had been sold to Rockmore Inc.

Noelle was opposed. Absolutely and wholly opposed. She didn't want her glorious, Victorian B and B turned into a soulless luxury resort made all of slate and glass. Need money. She didn't need to escape her life.

She didn't like that she had so much conflict with her mom now that her dad was gone.

Noelle's mother liked to remind Noelle that *her* name wasn't in this place. She wasn't a Holiday by blood, but by marriage, and she didn't want to stay in the little town forever. She wanted different things, and now that her husband was gone, she didn't have to keep living in this small town. She didn't have to confine her dreams to this mountaintop.

But Noelle's name *was* in this home, in this land. She wanted it more than anything. At the very least, she wanted the opportunity to buy her mother out. Of course, she didn't just have money. She would need time, a payment plan. She would need her mom to be patient. And to care, even a little bit about what mattered to Noelle.

It was just so frustrating. They had always had a somewhat contentious relationship, but with her mom bound and determined to sell the Christmas tree farm and Holiday House it had only gotten more strained.

Noelle didn't want to leave. She wanted to cling to this life, to all the warm, glowing memories she had here.

Life without her dad, life realizing that her parents' marriage hadn't been perfect, that her childhood wasn't quite so perfect, was just a little less cheerful than the life she'd grown up with. And if she wanted to cling to the past—with its warm glow of nostalgia and beautiful memories, who could blame her?

"You all right?" Melody asked as she handed her the latte.

"I'm fine," Noelle said. She forced a smile.

"No charge. You are officially bringing Christmas cheer to town, and I feel that you should be fairly compensated."

"Well, you don't need to do that," said Noelle.

But she would take it. Because she needed every penny that she could scrape up. She needed this year to be good.

That was the difficult thing. She needed the tourism. She realized that feeling grim and broody about advancements made in the town was… Ungrateful in a way. She needed people to want to come and stay at Holiday House. She needed an influx of travelers coming for Christmas. People who wanted Christmas trees, who wanted sleigh rides and to go through the elk preserve in wagons, she needed those people.

Because it was how she made money. It was how she continued to pay her employees. She might not be the owner of the B and B, but she managed it, taking a paycheck like everyone else with the rest of the earnings going to her mom.

Christmas was her stock in trade.

And the ski season was her best for obvious reasons.

But none of it mattered if everything she loved got leveled to make a new fancy hotel.

A strip mall.

The very idea. Strip malls in Snowflake Falls. What next?

The end of days.

She walked out of the coffee shop after bidding Melody a farewell, and looked down the festive main street again. And that was when she saw him.

He was taller than anyone else on the street, and he was dressed in black.

It felt like an aggressive block of darkness, right there in the middle of the well-lit street.

People bustled around him, in brightly colored knits, talking and laughing. In groups. He was singular, and there was nothing merry or bright about his expression.

But he was… He was the most beautiful man Noelle had ever seen. His hair was jet-black, as dark as midnight without stars. His eyes were the same sort of coal color, his jaw square, his mouth flat and severe. His shoulders were impossibly broad, and as he moved toward her, she felt her heart leap into her throat. Of course, he didn't see her. She was tucked beneath the awning of the coffeehouse, and she was… Well, she was a reindeer.

A brown blob in the midst of the seasonal glory.

He cut through the people like a blade, his every move efficient. Black jacket, black tie, black gloves, black pants, black shoes. She took in each and every detail as he moved closer and closer. Her heart felt like it would burst when he walked past. He didn't even flicker a glance.

She remained an unseen reindeer, standing there and sipping on her gingerbread latte.

Who *was* he?

She immediately started writing stories about him in her mind—how could she not. The town itself, and the citizens in it were always the same. Tourists were an endless source of fascination, but this man…even more so. Was he a man with a tragic backstory here to find his Christmas spirit. A widower? An investment banker from New York City who'd lost his way and needed a woman filled with the spirit of small-town Christmas to show him the right path?

Ha. Right.

He must be here with a wife, children. He was wearing gloves so she couldn't see whether or not there was a gold band on one of his large hands.

In many ways, he should look like anyone of the innumerable important executives who came to Snowflake Falls to ski, to eat local cuisine like bison Wellington and elk tenderloin. And yet, he didn't. There was something singular about him, and she couldn't put her finger on it.

You think he's hot?

She shimmied. She didn't think it was that. That would be very basic of her. Maybe she was basic.

She frowned into her latte. Then reached up and touched her antlers. She didn't think she was basic.

She cleared her throat and moved away from the entrance to the coffeehouse. She had to get back to Holiday House. Because the madness would be starting soon. She was manning the Christmas trees today, as that's where all the action would be. She did have new guests arriving, but the staff at the inn would be managing most of that.

Often, the running of the inn was her primary responsibility, as she lived in the house year-round. But when the festivities picked up around the rest of the property, she relied more heavily on her seasonal support staff.

Many of whom had been working at Holiday House for years.

The idea of them not having jobs anymore, the idea of them not being part of her life, it was absolutely unconscionable. Surreal.

She wouldn't let that happen.

"Time to sell Christmas trees," she said to herself as she marched down the street and back to her modest little car. She started to drive out of town, and up the winding, dirt road that led to Holiday House. Fat gray clouds loomed overhead, but they didn't bother her. This was her favorite time of year. When fall turned into winter, when the leaves finally gave their last gasp and fluttered to the ground.

When the ground froze and was covered in snow. She loved the snow.

Of course, with her father gone, it was up to her to keep the road to Holiday House plowed. Her father had bought an old, giant snowplow fifteen years earlier, and had used it to make sure that their guests could always get in and out of their property. Her father had thought of every wonderful little detail needed to make it the most glorious place to be during the cold winter months.

She didn't take the road that led to the B and B, rather she took the one that forked off and led to the little Christmas tree forest, which also boasted sleigh rides, hot chocolate, spiced cider, roasted chestnuts and various other forms of merriment.

The parking lot was already half full of people arriving from near and far to get their Christmas tree, and to have a festive experience.

She drove behind the parking lot to the employees-only access, and stopped in her small office, which was labeled: the North Pole.

She got out her card reader to help process transactions, and plugged it into her phone. Then she grabbed her light-up red nose and put it on, pressing the button so that it blinked merrily. She began to sing, a cheerful conglomeration of carols as she trundled about.

And that was when she saw a sleek black car winding its way into the parking lot. It was the strangest thing. She didn't have to see who was driving to know. In her gut.

Because the car was exactly like its owner. Sleek and sharp. Unerring. Dangerous.

What a strange thing to think.

She thought that he must be with a wife and children, why else would he be up here? Why else would he be getting a Christmas tree?

But then, he parked the car, and got out.

He was quite alone.

And he turned and began to walk toward her.

Rocco Moretti was not a man to suffer indignity. And this entire snow globe of a town was one indignity after another.

The roads were in a state of utter disrepair and the buildings were in a sorry state. And those sagging monstrosities were festooned from foundation to ridgeline with lights, ornaments and garlands. The entire thing was so sugary, it might as well be a gingerbread man's frosted armpit.

He hated it.

He hated Christmas.

He hated cheer.

He hated this place.

And yet, he had been advised that this was the smartest investment he could make at the moment.

He had already bought up swathes of land, and there was this one holdout. This rickety little Christmas tree farm.

The owner of the property had been communicating with him regularly about her terms, but had made it clear that her daughter had to sign off on the sale, or it couldn't occur.

Such were the terms of the property.

And right there, staring at him, was the tiniest little insult to injury he had ever seen.

A woman. With curly red hair, a blinking red nose, and antlers.

She might have been pretty, were she not ridiculous.

But then, he supposed that went for the entire town.

The glory and natural splendor surrounding it might have been awe-inspiring, but he could not overlook the adornment.

As was the same with the creature regarding him now.

He knew. Instinctively. That she must be the one. Of course she was. The one who was blocking his purchase of the last piece of land he needed in order to make the resort that he was bound and determined to have.

He knew all about the messy terms of wills. And he did not blame the woman desperate to offload this place left behind to her by her late husband.

Just as he had spent years cleaning out the mansion his mother had filled with her madness, he had also spent years trying to untangle the terms of her will.

Never a woman content with life, she had been quite like this whole town. Uselessly adorning each and every space with her influence. Collecting and collecting as if she would suddenly find the magic thing that brought fulfillment. Controlled chaos, she had called it, though he had never seen anything in it but chaos.

She had, though, proven that in her mind there was some form of control involved, by her utterly controlling last will and testament.

He must always keep building. You must always keep adding to the empire. New clutter onto the earth.

Or he must marry. Procreate. Before his thirty-second birthday. Worryingly close now.

A lovely parting gift from his mother, who had wanted to obsessively control everything for all time, and had succeeded in how she'd left the company to him, with a board of her own choosing there to make sure he complied.

But thankfully, he had it in hand. All of it.

He moved across the empty space, and approached the little indignity.

"Hello."

She only stared at him, aptly, as a deer caught in headlights.

"I am hoping that I might be able to trouble you for a place to stay tonight? This is Holiday House, yes?"

Women found his accent charming. He had learned English quickly. And had decided that it was good enough. Partly because the accent was of use to him.

"Oh, Holiday House is full tonight I'm afraid."

Well. He would solve that problem.

"A shame," he said.

"Do you… Are you with your family?"

"No," he said. "I'm only in town on business. Just myself."

"Oh. Right. Well, I suppose then that you don't need a Christmas tree."

He never needed a Christmas tree. He could think of nothing more vile. A dust catcher, shedding detritus all over the place.

"No thank you. I have no need. I have heard though that Holiday House is very beautiful. Is it all right if I drive up the road to see it?"

"Yeah. Of course."

"Thank you. I shouldn't like to have come so far to not even catch a glimpse of it."

"Where did you hear about it?"

"I'm quite certain it's on a list. Of rustic inns."

"Oh, yes. *Home and Garden*, *Town & Country* and *Countryside Magazine* all did features on it."

"*Countryside*. That must be it." Did she really think that he read periodicals? Like a geriatric man sitting in a doctor's waiting room?

Her nose blinked as she regarded him. Yes. She really might have been pretty, though it was very hard to say in what she was wearing. The knit brown dress clung to her curves, and her eyes were a russet gold. Her lips were pink and full, but the nose. And the antlers.

"My name is Noelle. Noelle Holiday."

"Nice to meet you," he said.

So this was the woman he needed to charm. The woman he needed to wrangle into signing the papers. He would have to make her an offer she couldn't refuse, and what better way than by charming her.

"And you are?"

"Rocco," he said. "Moretti."

"Well, it was nice to meet you, Mr. Moretti. Why don't you have a complimentary cup of cider?"

She turned away from him and picked up a ladle from a slow cooker, dipping it into steaming liquid and pouring it into a paper cup.

His lip curled involuntarily, and he tried to turn it into a smile. It was wholly unhygienic. And yet, he had no choice but to graciously accept it. Charm. He was aiming for charm.

"Many thanks. I will not keep you."

"Oh. You aren't a bother at all."

A *bother*. Imagine. Someone calling him a bother.

He took the cup, and got into his car, and then he drove

down the road, following the signs that would lead him to Holiday House. When he pulled up to it, everything in him recoiled. It was an old Victorian, as gaudy as everything else.

He got out of his car, holding the cup of cider. He poured it out onto the ground, and watched the steam rise from the frozen earth.

Then he crushed the cup in his fist.

He walked toward the front porch, and cast the waste into a bin that was placed there.

He brushed his hands off, and walked into the building. There was a young girl standing there, looking at the guest registry.

"I have a request."

CHAPTER TWO

By the end of the day, Noelle was exhausted, but she was still enervated by her encounter with him. Rocco ready. She was never going to see him again. He didn't need a Christmas tree, and the bed-and-breakfast was full. So, there was no reason that she would ever encounter him again.

Not ever.

Looking at him had been like being struck by lightning.

She had never experienced anything like it.

Of course, she had never experienced a day quite like today, and that was what she should be focusing on. The triumphant, rampant success of her grand opening day.

She hummed as she walked up the steps and into Holiday House.

The staff was already gone for the day, and it was quiet and cozy inside. She peered into the library, half expecting to see one of the guests in there reading or playing checkers. But there was no one there.

She frowned.

She was suddenly feeling exceptionally tired, though,

so while she would normally linger to try and see if the guests needed anything, she was feeling like she needed to lie down more than she needed anything else at the moment. So she decided to head straight to bed.

Her little bedroom was in the attic, with a bathroom added, and a kitchen area. So that there were times when she could be contained just to herself even when she had a house full of guests.

That was when she had taken over as innkeeper. When her parents had decided to spend more time away from Holiday House.

Before her dad had died.

That made her chest feel sore. She was already achy, and grumpy, and she didn't want a sore chest on top of it, so she redirected her thoughts. Instead, she went over to her record player, and gingerly selected a Christmas album that her grandmother had left to her. She placed it onto the table, and put the needle on the cherished, antique item. The Andrews Sisters' voices filtered into the room, and she saw to her bedtime routine. She brushed her teeth, washed her face and put on a long cotton nightgown.

In moments like this she could still imagine that she lived in a simpler time. One where both her parents were still with her. Maybe one where her grandma was still here, even. Or perhaps, back in midcentury. When times had been hard, certainly, but Holiday House had been a sanctuary, and no one had been coming to knock it over.

Wyoming would have felt so isolated then. So separate from everything going on in the world. Sometimes, she thought it was a miracle that everything was so connected nowadays. But not now. Right now, she wished that she could cut her little house off from the rest of the world, from the march of time.

She wished. She really did.

She lay down in bed with the record still playing, and slowly drifted off to sleep.

When she woke up, it was with a start. Her alarm hadn't gone off.

She turned and looked at it, and saw that it was blinking there in the darkness. It was still early, thankfully. At least, judging by how dim the light was coming through the window. She got up, and threw the curtains open. Outside there was nothing but white. A whole blanket of it. She was going to have to get up and plow the road.

Because it had been a whole blizzard. Unexpected this early in the year.

"Fiddlesticks," she said.

But then, she thought it was awfully funny that she had just been thinking last night about how nice it would be if she could take Holiday House and separate from the rest of the world right now.

But not right now. Not while she had guests, and employees that needed to get up here so that there could be breakfast and clean rooms, and myriad other things.

She charged out of bed and down the stairs, shoving her feet into her boots in the cloakroom, and grabbing a long coat. Then she shuffled out to the machine shed. She pulled the doors open, and went inside.

The old snowplow was parked, ever ready to fulfill its sacred duty. Clearing the roads so that guests would be able to get in and out. So that her employees would be able to get in and out.

She sighed and got into the driver's seat. And turned the key, always left in the ignition, because why not?

But nothing happened.

That had never happened before. Usually, the machine roared to life, and she was off.

But not this time.

She growled, and tried to turn the key again.

Nothing.

"Start," she commanded, but still, nothing happened. She tried and tried, but the machine was dead.

Great. That meant she was going to have to wait until the city got around to plowing the road up here.

Well, that was a disaster. That could take ages. She wasn't on the general map for plowing.

She huffed, and slid out of the snowplow, trudging back through the snow and up the front porch, back into the house.

She was struck yet again by how quiet it was. And then by the fact that her head felt heavy.

She could not be getting sick. Not on top of everything else. It was the damn season.

She groused into the kitchen, where she decided she better make some coffee. She opted to do it on the stovetop, rather than in the Mr. Coffee, trying to make it feel… Festive, maybe. She could always hunt through the freezer to see if there was anything easy to bake.

She found sugar cookies. Not exactly the boon she was hoping for.

But she set about getting those in, so that there were some pleasant smells that could fill the kitchen when the guests got up.

She was still wearing the oversized boots, and her nightgown, when she heard the first sound of footsteps on the stairs.

She was going to have to apologize. Because normally there would have been a whole breakfast. But it was only her.

And she had spent too long wrestling with a snowplow.

She walked into the entry room and stopped at the foot of the stairs. She could see a large, masculine hand on the railing, and she knew. The moment she saw those blunt fingers, she knew. Ridiculous, because the only other time she'd seen him he was wearing gloves.

But then he came into view, and there was no question. Rocco Moretti had somehow spent the night in this house last night.

"Good morning."

She looked up at him, her eyes wide. "What are you doing here?"

"I'm a guest in this establishment."

"It was booked," she said.

"Yes. It was. But I decided that I wanted to stay here, so I did."

"How?"

"I made arrangements."

She knew a sudden feeling of trepidation. She was snowed in with this man. Alone.

She was an innkeeper and she'd never thought too terribly much about guests and her safety or anything like that. She probably should have. But she'd grown up here and it had been an entirely safe situation one hundred percent of the time so she'd never worried.

Right now the whole room felt smaller. The whole house, the whole mountain. She looked at him and she shivered and it wasn't quite like fear. It was something she'd never really experienced before. A tension that filled her lungs and her limbs and made her feel like she might leap completely out of her skin.

"What arrangements exactly did you make?"

"I asked the girl who works at registration to give me the contact info for the guests who had booked rooms for the night."

"She can't do that. There's privacy and—"

"And they were entirely happy to take my alternative offer. Particularly when I told them that there was a plumbing issue at the bed-and-breakfast."

"And why did you tell them that?"

"Because I wanted to say here. I may have gone overboard."

"In what sense?"

"Well. I didn't have to buy out every room. But I did."

"I… I don't understand…"

"I offered the guests a refund, and then offered them free accommodation at my resorts in Jackson."

"Jackson!"

"Yes. They were happy to take the offer. The rooms are much more expensive than yours."

"How were you able to offer my guests a refund?"

"Well, I didn't give them a refund. I gave them money from my bank account. So the truth is, you will be paid twice. By them, and by me. I think you will find that to be satisfactory."

"I… Are you telling me that you're the only one here?"

"Yes."

"But that's… That's psychotic, you realize that, right?"

"What is psychotic about it? What I wanted was to be in control of this interaction."

"Why?"

"Because. Do you honestly not know who I am?"

"You said your name was Rocco."

"Yes. I'm Rocco Moretti. From Rockmore Incorporated. I am offering to buy this place."

Her stomach bottomed out. This was the man? Her personal nemesis. The man who was trying to ruin her life, her whole existence. It was probably why he'd stopped her in her tracks when she'd seen him on the street in town. Because she had sensed his innate evil.

"You're even worse than a serial killer," she spat. "You're a *property developer.*"

"I am that. A property developer, that is."

"Why are you… Why are you doing this?"

"Your mother told me that she was having no luck with you. I said that I would come speak to you. Also, I was informed that I needed to involve myself, as this was a very wise investment."

"It's not going to be an investment. Because I'm not going to agree to it."

"Really? You're not going to allow your mother to have this very generous offer of money?"

Rage filled her. Old rage from all the arguments she'd had with her mother about this very topic. She'd held herself back with her mom because she loved her mom. Relationships could be complicated without love being lost. But it was so, so difficult and it had made everything feel hard and anxious and she hated it.

And it was *his fault*.

"It's my dad's legacy," she said. "His family. Holiday House is our namesake. It means more than money."

"Not to your mother. Not at this point."

How dare he? With his whole handsome face, how dare he? She didn't even reduce her mother's actions to anything that mercenary. He didn't know them. He didn't know how grief had changed her mother and made it so she couldn't stand to be here. He didn't understand at all.

And maybe she didn't either, but at least she had context for her mom. He was just acting like she was a greedy monster. Or maybe she was projecting that because she was desperately trying to not think of her mom that way.

She gritted her teeth and faced him down, and ignored the quickening of her heartbeat—it was just anger anyway. "Don't talk about things you don't understand. She's trying to make a new way of life and that's been a source of tension with us, but you don't know her."

"I don't need to know your mother, or you, to know that eventually you'll come around. People always do. You can continue to struggle here or you can take a payout and go off to live a very happy life."

"No."

"The truth is, Miss Holiday, if you don't agree to this, all the sales fall through, not just yours. You will impact the well-being of your neighbors. Because I cannot build around—" he waved his hand "—this. And many other properties wish to sell. Can you imagine the goodwill that you will extinguish in this town if you ruin this deal for everyone?"

She sputtered, "That's manipulative."

He grinned. "I am quite manipulative. Or so it's been said." He lifted his hand from the railing on the banister, and rubbed his fingers together, as if touching it offended him.

"This place doesn't need a big modern resort," she said.

"Many would disagree with you."

"Well, those people don't have a sense of history."

"History. What do you think you're going to tell me

about history. You're an American. Your version of history on this continent is so new compared to my sense of history. I'm an Italian."

"Congrats on your frescoes, I guess. But you downplaying what this means to me is not going to change my mind."

"All right then, if not that, then what about this. I will offer you a very generous compensation package. And, if you do not want to leave here, I will offer you a job. Managing the hotel. Provided that I think you can handle it."

"I don't want to work for you. I work for myself. In my family-owned business. If you can't understand why that's different…"

"I understand." He walked all the way down the steps, and turned around the room, looking around them. "This is… Quaint. But you must admit, the appetite for such a place has never been lower than it is now."

Suddenly, she was seized by the urge to sneeze. She couldn't fight it. She inhaled, and then rocked forward hard, covering her face as best she could.

When she looked up, he had drawn back, his hands touching the collar of his suit jacket. The man was in a suit at six in the morning.

"Are you well?"

"I'm feeling a bit under the weather," she said.

"That is unfortunate."

"Well. The chores will not wait for anyone. I need to figure out how to fix my snowplow."

"If you worked for me, the chores would wait. You would have sick leave."

"Well, I wouldn't today, Mr. Moretti."

"You think not?"

"Yeah. I think not."

"I'm not sure exactly what game you're playing."

"Well, remind me again what game you're playing," she said. "Because I'm curious. What exactly was your name again?"

"I came up here to convince you that this place is not where you want to be."

"Ironic," she said. "Because now you're stuck here."

"Excuse me?"

"I can see that you're the kind of man who is used to getting his way. The kind of man who thinks he's in control of everything. But I regret to inform you, Mr. Moretti, that you don't control the weather."

CHAPTER THREE

ROCCO LOOKED AROUND the space, he felt an increasing sense of discomfort. There were things *everywhere*. The decor could best be described as dust catching. He was not amused. Nor was he impressed. The sooner a place like this was torn to the ground, all the better as far as he was concerned. It was the antithesis to everything that he created in his resorts. He strived for clean lines, for minimalism. Modern luxury, with no nonsense.

This place was entirely nonsense. And now, this… Sneezing creature in the nightgown was telling him that he was stuck here?

Then there was…her.

She was not dressed as a reindeer just now. But her red hair remained untamed, and her face was dotted with freckles. Her sweater was chunky and had a snowflake pattern and she had eyeshadow with glitter. She was maximalist, as a human.

And she was beautiful. Like everything he'd never wanted wrapped into an enticing package that should be as off-limits as it was forbidden.

He was not accustomed to that. The lure of the forbidden. His life was controlled. His space was his own and everything in it had been put there specifically by him.

This place was not his. The weather was not his to control.

And the way he felt about her was like all of these things that were so foreign to him wrapped up in lush, soft-looking skin.

What was this? If they were unresolved issues from his childhood come back to haunt him, he'd happily skip them.

It said a lot about him, perhaps, that he was suddenly afraid his childhood torment had manifested in his adult years as a kink for a woman who seemed to represent *chaos*.

There was a psychological breakthrough.

That which he could not control as a child, he wanted to screw as a man.

He would rather never ponder that again.

"I do not do *stuck*."

"Well, maybe not, but that does seem to be the situation. Stuck."

"What exactly do you mean?"

He went to the front door, and opened it. And saw that outside was nothing but white. It wasn't just that there was snow on the ground, it was falling thick and hard all around them, and the air was misty.

It was a total whiteout. He turned around to face her. "What do you normally do in a situation like this?"

"Normally?" She wrinkled her nose. "Well, normally,

I plow my way out. But the problem is that there is no normal right now, because my snowplow won't start."

"Your snowplow won't start?"

"No—" She heaved back again, and wrenched forward with a giant sneeze. "No," she said. "My snowplow won't work. I've never had that happen before, I'm not a mechanic."

"How long do you think this will be?"

"I don't know. This is going to be part of the reality if you are buying property up here. If you really think that this is going to be where your big, sleek luxury resort is."

"I was easily able to lure your guests from here to my place."

"For free," she said. "And when you told them this place was a mess."

"This place is a mess. How long do you suppose it will be until you actually find yourself with some sort of insurmountable plumbing issue."

"I won't. Because it's actually in a better state than that."

A timer went off in the other room.

"Hang on."

She went through the door, and he followed her. There was a kitchen, large and clean, more modern than the rest of the house, updated he thought, to comply with code. So there was that. Not that it mattered in the grand scheme of things, since this place would not remain standing once he purchased this plot of land, but... Good for him now. Because otherwise he would starve.

She leaned down, and opened up the oven, covering her hand with a cloth, and taking out a sheet with cookies on it.

"What is that?"

"It's… Breakfast. Of a variety. I was trying to get something on the table as quickly as possible. Since I was out fiddling with the snowplow for so long."

"Did you make the dough this morning?"

"No," she said.

"I don't eat leftovers."

"You don't… You don't eat leftovers?"

He shook his head. "No."

He wouldn't explain himself to her. He didn't have to do that. That was what he chose to do with his money. He chose to make himself into an island. He chose to craft his surroundings into something that worked for him, and he did not have to explain it.

"I don't know that I have… All that much here."

He went to the fridge and opened it, and took out a carton of eggs.

"This will suffice."

She suddenly looked alarmed, then moved away from him, the tray of cookies and the oven, and sneezed again.

"I do not wish for you to prepare the food anyway. I will make some eggs."

"Do you know how to do that?"

"How hard can it be?"

"You don't know how to cook eggs?"

"I haven't done it before, that doesn't mean that I don't know how."

She sneezed again.

"You are unwell. I do not wish to have you sporing around my food."

She sputtered. "I am not...*sporing*."

"You are," he said. "Sadly. For both of us."

"What do you want me to do?"

"Out," he said.

She obeyed him but not before grabbing a pot and two cups. But her general obedience was surprising, because she had been nothing but curmudgeonly from the moment they had encountered one another this morning.

She was quite ungrateful for what he was attempting to do.

Most people were happy to take the check. Living in places like this was not easy. There were few rewards for working as hard as people like her were working. There were few rewards for living such a hardscrabble life. In truth, as he expanded his resort empire, resistance was so unusual that he didn't even have an inbuilt method for dealing with dissenters. Usually, all he had to do was make it clear that he was sincere in the money that he was offering, and people took the check, and gave him the land.

This sort of thing was... Unwell. Mentally unstable behavior, in his opinion. People who were so attached to a specific place or thing that they couldn't bear to get rid of it... There was something wrong with them.

MILLIE ADAMS   37

He looked around the kitchen, uncertain about where he might find a pan. He opened the drawers until he noticed one under the stovetop, and inside found a skillet. He was resourceful. It galled him to have to look up a recipe for eggs.

Surely it was *eggs*. What else could it entail?

But he did search for a recipe, because if nothing else, he was a perfectionist. And he found there was slightly more to it than he had imagined.

But there was a level of control with food that he required, and at least this would allow him to have that.

He spent longer than he would like to admit looking for a mixing bowl, and a whisk, but then he followed the instructions on the website that he had found on his phone, and set about to the task of scrambling the eggs.

He grimaced as he did so, but before he knew it, he had a dozen eggs scrambled. He portioned them out so that he had the lion's share, and she had a bit, and then he added a cookie to her plate. Clearly she had been happy enough to eat the cookies.

He walked out of the kitchen, and did not see her. He moved down the hall, both plates in his hands, and finally saw a dining room, where she was sitting at the end of an ornate dining table with a lace tablecloth. Tablecloths made no sense to him. Better to wipe the hard surface of the table than add cloth to the top of it that you would have to launder after.

"Here," he said, putting a plate in front of her.

"Scrambled eggs and a cookie," she said.

"Yes," he said.

"Well, there's coffee in this carafe."

He was reasonably comfortable with that. He liked his coffee black and strong, and this would suffice.

"Why don't you eat leftovers? Are you too fancy?"

"I am not... Fancy."

"Then why? It sounded like an incredibly snobbish and wasteful mindset. Anyway, they weren't leftovers. They were frozen preshaped cookies ready to bake."

"Oh," he said. "That's fine."

"So why don't you eat leftovers?"

"Does it not bother you if you don't know the age of food?"

"I've never thought about it."

"You've clearly never eaten anything past its expiration date, then."

"Um... Well, no. I mean, I've definitely found things in the fridge that shouldn't have been there."

"Occasionally," he pressed.

"Yes, a couple of times."

"Yes. You might feel differently if it were a more frequent occurrence."

And that was all she would get.

"You aren't going to convince me to sell. We are at an impasse."

"Do you really think that's fair? Your mother is desperate for you to make a different choice."

"She's not desperate. She's grieving, and she's not

doing it very well. She just wants to make it like he wasn't here. And that's not fair."

"Noelle," he said, her name strange on his lips. "Surely you must realize this is a foolish thing to go up against me."

"There is no against. I won't sell to you. And that's my choice."

"Surely you must have a price."

"Build somewhere else. Why does it matter so much to you that you have this?"

"Because I must keep building," he said. "And this is an excellent way to do that."

"Why do you have to keep building?"

"To expand my business."

"Aren't you like… One of the richest men in the world?"

"You didn't even know who I was when I introduced myself to you yesterday, and now you're talking about my status and wealth?"

"I googled you while you were making eggs."

"All right then. Yes. I am."

"Then why?"

"I must expand the company every year by two percent or it dissolves. Those are the stipulations of my mother's will."

"Really?"

"Yes."

"You just lose ownership of it if you don't…do that. Who's in charge of it?"

"There's a board. Who of course would love it if I lost control, because it would mean that they could have it. And I will not allow a board of my mother's enablers to have their way."

"Do you love the business?"

"Love the business? What does that mean?"

"I love Holiday House. I love it. I can feel the legacy of my family here. Memories of my father. I love this place. It means the world to me. Do you feel that way about Rockmore?"

"No," he said. "I don't."

"Then why does it matter?"

"Because I refuse to lose."

"What would you be losing?"

Why not tell her? This was an aberration and he was forced to exist in it, so why not talk to her? This creature he would never have spoken to as part of his normal life. Why not…indulge?

He did not do chaos or indulgence in his real life, and here he was, steeped in both. The snow making a mockery of the idea he'd ever had power over anything of note. It was perhaps more that his life had not encountered an act of God before now.

"The game. I do not cede control, *cara*."

She wrinkled her nose, and in spite of himself he found it…charming.

Had he ever been charmed before?

"You do not cede control or eat leftovers. So interesting."

She sneezed again. And he fought against his own distaste for anything germ related.

"You must go to bed," he said. "You are unwell."

"I've certainly been *more* well," she said, sounding flat.

"What would you do if you had a place full of guests?"

She looked slightly helpless then. "I don't know." She squinted. "I refuse to thank you."

"I do not require your thanks, though it is something to think about."

"Is there any way that you can… Stop ever?" she asked as she picked up her coffee, as if she was going to take it to bed with her.

"What do you mean?"

"I just mean… Is there any way… Another way that lets you stop the expansion?"

He mulled telling her this truth, as it was…like all things with his mother it was incomprehensible, and he found it humiliating in a strange way. Exposing the ridiculousness of the woman who had birthed him, raised him. But it was also the truth of her, and of his life, so what could be done?

"Yes," he said. "There is."

"What's that?"

"I have to get married. And have a child."

She blinked. "Your mom was kind of controlling."

"You have no idea," he said.

"Well, can you understand that I don't want my mother controlling me?"

"I can. Except this decision controls her also. As long as you have this place, she is tethered to it. It determines what sort of life she can live. My mother is dead. She is controlling me from the grave. Because she can no longer control everything in life."

She walked out of the room, and left him there to contemplate his eggs. He could see that he was in an uphill battle. When a person could not be manipulated with money, he simply had no idea how to proceed.

He wasn't used to being at loose ends. At least, not these days. During his childhood, he had often spent hours alone. Moving about in darkness. Living in tainted luxury where only one space was ever sacred.

His bedroom had been a necessary refuge. One that he had controlled fiercely.

The old manner home had secret passages, and they had allowed him to move through the walls, to access different portions of the house. So that he didn't have to walk down the cluttered hallways. But still, there were no other spaces in the house that his mother had not claimed with her illness.

He didn't like being trapped somewhere. It was too reminiscent of that time in his life. It was too reminiscent of days he would rather forget.

How he loathed it.

It was drafty in this house. And it was old.

Even though the manor home he had grown up in had been much more stately than this, it had still been old.

And old equaled chill. Damp. Particularly where he had lived in the Italian Alps.

Many people thought of warmth when they thought of Italy. Not so where he had resided.

He could well remember winters where they had been blanketed in a deluge of snow. He had never liked it. It had increased that feeling of being isolated in the walls of their home.

And so it was now.

But he was concerned about his charge.

She had become his charge, somehow.

He did not fear illness, but he had a preoccupation with cleanliness and the control of said cleanliness, because in his childhood home he'd had no control of his surroundings. Still, it had become a fixation on cleanliness, and this was pushing against his comfort level.

But he would simply wash his hands more often.

There was no one else to care for her.

He had never cared for another person before. He had never had occasion to.

He had spent his life caring for himself. As a child it had often felt like a matter of survival. There had been two elderly household employees who worked for his mother, and they handled meals, such as they were.

As an adult, it felt like a luxury. To be able to care for himself, more or less, without the interference of his mother making it more challenging. Because that was how it had been. Ever and always. If he could find a way to ease things for himself, she would often make it more challenging with her impossible demands and needs. She wanted control. Over everything. Including him. When he had stopped being malleable, when he had stopped being a child, she had found all that much more difficult.

He decided that the best way forward would be to build the fire. So, he was going to take charge. And that was how it would be.

CHAPTER FOUR

HER HEAD WAS POUNDING. Or perhaps it was just a pounding happening outside. It was difficult to say. She sat up, feeling groggy, and wondered if she had fallen asleep, or if she had just drifted out of consciousness for a moment.

She looked at the clock. Only twenty minutes had passed since she had come upstairs. It was possible that she had dozed. She felt terrible. She rolled out of bed, and went over to the window, and what she saw outside made her brows rise.

He was out there. Chopping wood.

In a suit.

Without thinking, she opened up the window. "What are you doing?" She looked down at the man himself, knee-deep in the snow wearing clothing that probably cost more than she had ever seen in her life.

"Go back to bed," he said, looking up at her ferociously.

"Are you practicing to cut me into tiny pieces and take the house from me, or…?"

"I am not practicing the fine art of dismemberment.

I am cutting firewood. That I might warm the library, seeing as you have a chill."

"Oh," she said. "Why that is very kind of you. Suspiciously so."

"I hate to be suspicious."

"Somehow, I don't think that you do."

"I promise, I do not wish to murder you."

"Well, *very* reassuring." But then she felt not so great, so as amazing as the sight below was, she ended up making her way back to her bed.

She must have dozed again, because when she opened her eyes, the door to the bedroom was open, and it had grown darker outside. "Here," said a very masculine voice.

She looked over. He was standing there holding a tray with a steaming bowl and a steaming mug.

"What is it?"

"I opened a can of soup. And I made tea."

"Oh. Well, that's very nice of you."

Still suspicious.

"Yes. It was." He sounded pleased with himself, if a bit surprised.

She looked around. "I don't want to be ungrateful, but I find that I don't really relish the idea of trying to eat soup in bed."

"I have built a fire," he said.

"Excellent," she said. "Maybe I'll eat down in the library. It's only a cold."

She sneezed.

"Yes. Let us… I will carry the food. If you sneeze whilst carrying the tray it is likely to cause a small disaster."

"I am nothing if not a small disaster." She got out of bed, clutching a tissue in her hand, and followed him out of the room.

"Are you?" he asked.

"Am I what?"

"A small disaster."

He was asking about her now? What strange dimension had she fallen into. He was cutting wood and caring for her and acting like…he cared about getting to know her, which couldn't be true.

She looked at his face—dear God he was handsome—and she tried to get a handle on what he was thinking. What he felt about anything.

He was a mystery, and she didn't think it was only because she had limited experience with men. He was… something else.

No leftovers. No experience making soup.

So cold in so many ways and yet…he'd taken care of her, so he wasn't entirely cold.

"It feels like it. Because how else have I found myself in this position? Snowed in on a mountaintop with a nonworking snowplow and a very large stranger who clearly wishes to be rid of me."

"Did I *say* that I wish to be rid of you?"

"You're trying to buy me out." She felt it prudent to point out—to him and to herself—that even though he'd been kind to her while she was sick he was still trying to fundamentally upend her way of life.

"That has nothing to do with my desires for you either way."

She felt a little bit warm suddenly. That was an odd collection of words for him to use in regard to her. Definitely a collection of words no man had ever used in her presence.

"Well, I'm only me. For all that it's worth."

"And you want to stay here. I can't say that I fully understand."

She led the way toward the library, but stopped at the entrance to the kitchen. She looked inside. It looked like… A disaster had occurred.

Not a small one.

"What happened in here?"

"I won't leave it," he said.

"You opened a can of soup and made tea?" It looked like he'd performed surgery.

Every cabinet was opened, and there was water all over the place. The microwave was open, and she could see a noodle hanging down from the top of it.

"I have never made soup before."

"You opened a can and warmed it up. That's technically not making soup. Not trying to be unkind."

He scowled. "I am not accustomed to doing such tasks."

"I bet you never cut wood either. But you didn't cut

your hand off. So there's that. Have you ever boiled water before?" she asked him.

"Of course not," he said. "What occasion would I have had to boil water?"

"I don't know. We don't actually know each other. We're just stuck here, on a mountaintop. Because that's the way things are." She looked around. "Would you like a hand cleaning up?"

"Of course not. You're unwell. I want you to go sit and eat your soup. I will clean."

"I bet you don't know how to clean either."

His expression went thunderous. "I know how to clean."

She went into the library, and sat in a large chair, propping her feet up on a tufted ottoman. He handed her the tray with her soup and tea. It really was a nice gesture, all things considered. What a strange man he was. Not that she had any experience of men to compare him to anybody else. Not that she had any experience with men. She loved her hometown, but the men here were boring. She'd known them for too long, and when you'd known a man when he was thirteen there was little to make him interesting in his twenties.

And the good-looking, exciting men that came to town were either with their wives or husbands. That was just how it went. And there was a parade of very handsome men. Wealthy, sophisticated. Completely out of reach.

He was the first eligible man she had met around here.

If you could call a towering inferno of rock, rage and capitalism *eligible*.

Actually, she didn't even know if the eligible bit was true. Maybe he was engaged to the woman who would free him from his life of eternal expansion. Though she couldn't actually get a read on if he wanted that or not.

He definitely didn't seem to like being under the control of anyone or anything, but she had no idea what he thought about that versus finding a wife. She had no real idea what he thought about anything.

Though she was unhappy to admit he was clearly more complex than she'd initially thought. When she'd told him he was worse than a serial killer.

He wasn't, obviously. Since, in fairness, a serial killer wouldn't have nursed her back to health.

She picked up a saltine cracker and ducked it into her chicken soup.

She heard a great commotion going on in the next room, and she ignored it deliberately as she chewed on the corner of the cracker.

He reappeared about twenty-five minutes later.

"Are you well?" he asked.

"I'm fine. Are you engaged?"

He looked stunned by the question. "No," he said.

"Just wondering. I didn't think you were."

"I'm not certain how to take that."

"Oh, at face value, I would suggest. There was no hidden meaning. I was only curious. Plus you know you mentioned that whole thing about your mother, and marriage and a child. I thought maybe you'd taken steps toward that. I thought it was funny, because you're the first eligible bachelor that I've ever met in this town—" She swallowed some of her tea, and her throat felt wretched. Then, she felt embarrassed, because she shouldn't have exposed herself in quite that way.

"I am not engaged. *Eligible* is another question."

She laughed. "That's funny, because I was thinking the same thing."

"Have you got a husband?"

"If you talked to my mother then you already know that I don't. And you already know that some of her objection to me staying in this place is that I'm not going to meet anybody." She frowned. "One of the worst things about my mother wanting to get out of here so quickly is that it makes me feel like she never actually loved our lives. That she never actually loved my father in quite the way that I thought she did."

He only stared at her. There was no kinship there. No understanding.

"Well, wouldn't you feel that way if you found out that your mother was desperate to escape the life that she had lived with your father?"

"I never knew my father."

"Oh. I'm sorry."

"It's fine. It means nothing to me."

"So you were raised just by your mother?"

"Yes."

"In Italy?"

"Yes. In Italy."

"Really only two people here. We might as well make small talk."

It was just a polite thing to do. And yes, sometimes the out-of-towners, the people who came from cities, they resisted it. They didn't really understand what the point of it was, or what she was doing in trying to engage them, but she was insistent on giving her guests the small-town experience. Plus she just liked meeting new people and hearing about their lives.

She loved her life.

But it was the only one she'd lived. Obviously. But she'd just never...gone away to college or lived in another state or tried life in a city or anything. So a window into how someone else lived always fascinated her.

"I was raised here," she said. "Obviously. This place has been in my father's family for generations. It means the world to me. My grandmother lived here as the innkeeper until she passed away, when I was fifteen. Then for a couple of years we had somebody else live here as a caretaker, and when I turned eighteen, I took the job."

"And your parents lived where?"

"Oh, in town. We worked up here, but we lived closer to things. My mother already sold that house. To pay for her new condo in Florida. She likes it better where the sun shines all the time. But I don't."

"Have you ever lived where the sun shone all the time?"

"No."

"Then how do you know you will not like it?"

"Did you think that you would like making soup?" she asked.

"No."

"Sometimes you just know things."

They were silent for a moment. She wanted to push him. Press for more information, but she also didn't want to cause drama.

"So," she said. "You're from Italy."

"Yes," he said slowly, as if answering questions was a particularly strange thing for him. "From the Italian Alps. My mother is from a very old, very wealthy family, and she had more money than sense. She got herself pregnant when she was older. And decided to never reveal to anyone the identity of her baby's father. That was me."

"Oh. But she... She was very wealthy." Which she imagined didn't fix everything, but it had to fix a lot of things.

"My great-great-grandfather was a count, and also a real estate developer. The company had passed through two generations of our family before going to my mother. She did quite well in aspects of the job. Though, in the end, she receded from public life, and did most of her business online. Far before it was trendy for people to work remotely."

"Oh."

"There," he said, his tone definitive. "That is my story."

"That's *not* your story. That's a biography of your

company, mostly. Why did she end up leaving you instructions like she did in her will? Why did you end up in that position?"

"She was eccentric," he said.

That only piqued her curiosity further. Because eccentric was not a word she would ever use to describe him. So how had he come to be? And what had she been like really?

"It sounds like it."

"At the end of her life she did not leave the house at all. We were very isolated. She liked to control everything." He stood there in the doorway, something reticent about his stance. "If I were a psychologist I would suggest that something traumatic happened to her. But I do not know."

"Oh."

Well. That wasn't fun eccentric.

He hesitated before speaking. "We were quite cut off from the rest of the world for the past decade of her life. It made things difficult. But she always wanted to maintain the level of control that she had in her home. And she wanted to make sure that she controlled me after she died. Hence the will."

"I see." She felt she had to stop saying *oh*. But she didn't really know what else to say to this...list of facts.

She could sense that he had compassion for his mother, but there was also anger. A lot of anger. She couldn't really blame him. She was frustrated that her mom was trying to control her life. That she was trying to take this from her. She could imagine that he didn't feel any better about it.

"Did you have staff?"

"Two members of staff. That had been with my mother for all of her life. They were elderly."

"So that's why you don't know how to make food."

"Yes."

"But you clean."

"I'm a man who has lived on my own for any number of years. And while I am happy to order food, I like to keep my surroundings in a certain level of order."

"You don't have a cleaning staff."

"I do. But you cannot have your home too clean."

He looked around the cluttered library, his expression one of pure disdain.

"I take it you don't like shelves packed full of books? And figurines and doilies?"

"No," he said.

"I do. It's history. Knowledge. A lot of this was collected over the years by my family. It's important to us. It's part of our story."

"I will never feel that way about dust catchers, I'm afraid. They do not appeal to me."

"Sorry," she said. "That's a little bit intense."

"I'm a little bit intense."

She laughed. "What are you going to eat?"

"I made myself a bowl of soup. I ate it before I delivered yours."

"Well, when I noticed the mess you really should have

given yourself that credit. You made two bowls of soup. That's why it was such a disaster."

He didn't even seem on the verge of cracking a smile. What a tough customer. He was gorgeous. Truly, the most incredible man she had ever seen in person, but he would be impossible to try to deal with on a daily basis. Or at all. Ever. She didn't know how anyone dealt with him. Maybe nobody really did. Maybe that was the perk of being a billionaire. Nobody really ever contended with you. They just sort of let you exist around them.

"I'm attached to this place," she said. "I love it."

"I consider that adjacent to mental illness," he said.

She gaped at him. "I'm sorry, what? People love their familial homes. You yourself were just talking about the fact that you descended from a long line of important people, you had a familial home, and a business. How is what I feel for this bed-and-breakfast different than that?"

"It simply is," he said.

"But that doesn't make any sense."

"It can cross a line, into foolishness. When you are so attached to a place that you begin to hurt yourself in the pursuit of hanging onto it, when you love things so much that you would choose them over the people in your life, then yes, I do believe it is adjacent to mental illness. And I will not apologize for that."

"You should. It's offensive."

"I don't care if I'm offensive."

She felt heat beneath his words, he was personally upset about this. Personally inflamed by it.

"You think that me refusing to sell this place because my mother wants the money is me choosing a place over my family."

"Yes," he said.

"It isn't. I would pay her for it. I would buy it from her. But I either have to be able to get financing, or I have to be able to make payments to her. I need time. Also, I can't give her the exorbitant sum that you are. But isn't there a point where wanting more money is simply greed?"

"Isn't there a point where wanting stuff is simply accumulation?"

"I don't understand the difference in the two things."

"Money can afford you the opportunity to live somewhere with a view that you like. You can live in a sleek, clean surrounding, and money allows you to do that comfortably. With good food. Without the worry of scarcity."

"My mother is hardly living in scarcity. If that's what she told you, then it is a gross exaggeration. What she wants is to be done living what I consider to be a modest life. But I'm not done with it. I love it."

"Things are not inherently valuable. They have only the sentiment that you attached to them. You can simply carry a memory in your heart."

"Haven't you ever heard that home is where your heart is?"

"I have never had that experience."

There was something there that he wasn't sharing. And she wasn't sure that she needed him to. Nor was she sure she even wanted to hear about it. There was no point getting to know this man. Who was in opposition to her in every way. Who was insulting. Who was a threat to her way of life.

"Thank you for the soup," she said. "And the crackers. But I'm tired and I'm going to go to bed."

"All right then," he said.

She stood up, and brushed past him, and as she did, she stumbled slightly, he grabbed her arm, and steadied her, and she found herself looking up, way up, into the fathomless depths of his black eyes.

Her throat froze, going tight. Her heart slammed itself against her breastbone like it was attempting a jailbreak. He smelled… Well, she could hardly smell, but from what she could tell he smelled of wood smoke and skin. She had never been close enough to smell someone else's skin.

"Oh," she said. "I think I'm delirious."

She practically windmilled away from him, and carried on up the stairs. And then she lay down on the bed, her hand pressed to her heart.

That was insanity. And she was not going to indulge it.

CHAPTER FIVE

THE SNOW DID not let up. The next day, it had piled up even higher than it had the day before. She called the local department of transportation and was told they couldn't plow up her way yet, as long as it wasn't a safety issue.

"No, we're just fine," she sighed, hanging up the phone.

But the good news was, her cold was much, much better. The bad news? Was when she heard Rocco sneeze.

"Oh, *no*," she said.

"I'm fine," he growled, his voice much rougher than it had been the day before.

"No, you aren't," she said.

She didn't need to know him well to know in advance he would be the worst patient imaginable.

"I never get sick," he said. "I am fastidious about germs."

She pinched the bridge of her nose. "As you pointed out yesterday, I was *sporing* in your vicinity."

"You can't get sick that quickly, can you?"

"I don't know," she said. "I'm not an expert in anything. Except maybe home remedies."

"We need a home remedy for your snowplow. So that we can get out of here."

Great. His response to this illness she very obviously had no control over was going to be him being growly at her.

How nice for her.

"Well, I am more likely to be able to help your cold than I am to deal with the carburetor or the starter or whatever is happening with that thing."

"*You* did this to me," he said.

She threw her hands into the air. "You just said that you don't get sick that quickly, or ever."

"Well, now I'm convinced *it was you.*"

She huffed. "Maybe it was somebody you encountered on your travels."

"I travel in a private plane."

"I don't know. Maybe it was your driver."

He looked stormy, and she went to get a cup of coffee from the kitchen.

"*You* seem well," he said.

And he seemed petulant, but she did not say that.

"I am," she agreed. "Which is good news for you. Because that means that you're probably going to be just fine in not very long."

"I should hope so. Also, I sincerely doubt that this is going to diminish me in any way."

"Oh. Do you?"

"I have business to attend to, I don't have time to be ill."

Of course, of course he had been working the whole time he was here.

"You know, sometimes getting sick is your body's way of telling you to rest."

"That is the stupidest thing I have ever heard." He was thunderous, and he was ridiculous, and still handsome and she had no idea what she was supposed to do with this—the feeling inside her—or him.

Though one thing she was sure of was that no matter how handsome he was, he was annoying.

"Sorry. I'll try to talk to myself next time. I'm sure that I can come up with something even better."

"Why are you so relentless?"

"Am I relentless?" He looked infuriated. He looked ill.

"Go sit in the library. I'll start a fire, and then I'll bring you something to eat."

He felt terrible. He was quite certain that he felt much worse than she had, his whole body beginning to shake as hot and cold flashes racked him.

This was absurd. He couldn't remember the last time he was sick. Well. He could. But he deliberately pushed the memory aside.

Because he didn't want to think about being alone in his bedroom. He didn't want to think about going into the kitchen to try and find someone to get him some food. He didn't want to think about climbing over endless stacks of garbage and expired products…

So he didn't.

Except his head was swimming, and whenever he closed his eyes he saw his childhood bedroom. And then the rest of the house.

He stood, enraged when the floor dared tilt beneath his feet.

"What are you doing?" Noelle asked, sticking her head into the room.

"I'm going to lie down for a moment."

"You seem… You seem feverish."

She crossed the room, and before he could pivot away from her, she pressed her hand to his forehead. "You're burning up. You need to go lie down."

"I just said that I was on my way to go lie down," he growled. He could still feel where her hand had touched his face, cool and comforting. Softer than he would've expected.

Earlier, when he had grabbed her arm to steady her when she had lost her balance, he had felt a bolt of sensation, one that he was intent on denying now.

He did not engage in indiscriminate physical affairs. He certainly wasn't going to engage in one in this house. In this state. But this creature. He tried to picture her with the antlers, but he was unsuccessful. All he could see was her freshly scrubbed face, her sweet smile, her freckles.

"I'll help you," she said.

"I don't need help," he said.

"I think you do," she said, beginning to propel him from the room and up the stairs.

"You're tiny," he said as she grabbed hold of his arm and tried to move him.

"I'm not that tiny," she said, sniffing angrily.

And right then, he felt like he had been hit in the side of the head. Not from illness, from something else entirely.

This chaos, and she was chaos. This tornado of desire that was wholly and entirely connected to her.

"You are," he said.

"I think you're ridiculous."

She shifted, bringing herself beneath his arm, and that was when he felt like he had been shot clean through with an arrow.

It was like the illness itself had stripped away something. Himself, maybe, because all he could see was how beautiful she was. It didn't matter that the first time he had seen her she had been dressed like a reindeer. And it didn't matter that her house was ridiculous, or that she was a barrier to getting what he wanted, which normally made someone his enemy and nothing more.

Suddenly, she was a beautiful enigma.

"I think my fever might be dangerously high," he said.

"Well, that's concerning. But I can take your temperature."

He narrowed his eyes. "How?"

She started laughing. "Oh, don't worry about that. There's no reason to get that medical. I'll just put it under your tongue." She guided him to the room that he was staying in. And then she disappeared.

He was suddenly overly warm, and he stripped his shirt off, then went to the closet where he had deposited his belongings earlier, and took out a pair of sweatpants. He put them on, then lay down on the top of the bed. This illness had come on like a freight train. And entirely without his permission. He was incensed. As he did not allow for things like this. And yet. Nothing was going the way that he wanted it to.

You cannot control the weather.

Hell and damn. He had controlled plenty enough for a good while now. Why was everything suddenly out of his hands?

"Oh!"

She sounded immediately like a heroine from an old movie, offended and horrified all at once, when she stepped into the room and saw him lying there on the bed, bare-chested.

"I thought that I would get comfortable," he said.

"Of course," she said.

Then she seemed to avert her gaze as she came to the bed with a thermometer in hand. She knelt down beside him. "Open your mouth."

She slipped the thermometer inside, and he knew a sense of warmth and care like he had never known before.

He'd been sick as a child, of course. But there had been no hand on his forehead. There had been no concerned figure by his bedside. Maybe there would have been if he hadn't shut them all out. If he hadn't put so much distance between himself and his mother even then.

There was no way to know.

And he could not ask her now.

She put her hand on his forehead again. And he was... Undone. "You are very warm," she said. "I wasn't this feverish. I'm concerned that you have something worse."

"It wouldn't dare," he said.

"The virus?"

"Yes," he said.

"You are formidable, but I don't think you're that formidable. Sorry."

"All tremble in my wake."

Even he knew he was being ridiculous at this point.

"I am very sorry that you have been so sorely offended," she said. "But you have to stop talking, because you're ruining the temperature."

He stopped. It was an old-fashioned thermometer. Glass. And it took minutes for it to get his temperature. He almost thought she was using it on purpose. To keep him quiet. But he didn't mind, because there was something somewhat comforting about having her there, kneeling beside him, holding the thermometer.

"Yes. You are quite feverish," she said. "It's over one hundred. That is concerning."

"Now what are you doing?"

"I'm going to get you some medicine. I'm going to get you soup."

"What if I don't want to eat it in bed?"

"I'm going to ask that you eat in bed," she said. "Because I don't want to have to maneuver you up and down the stairs every time. You can eat at the writing desk if you like. Otherwise, I'll bring you a little bed tray to prop your food up on."

She fluttered out of the room, and when she returned a little while later, she was fully supplied with anything he might need.

He took the medicine, and began to eat, but he felt like his thoughts were only becoming less and less clear. His throat hurt, his body beginning to ache fiercely. He soon fell asleep, but he was very aware that cool cloths were continually changed on his face.

He woke up when the sun was setting.

"How are you?"

"I've been better," he said.

"Well, I'm going to keep watch. Because… Well. I'm worried about you. I've been checking on you every twenty minutes or so, which is maybe silly but… I don't know. You just seem very unwell."

Had anyone ever worried about him before? It scraped him raw, and he forgot why he ever held anything back. He forgot why he had fashioned himself into a fortress, because it was all too easy to forget the life he'd built in these past twenty years.

It was easy, right now, for him to believe there had only been his childhood, and this moment. Like all the space in between had evaporated. Been swallowed whole by his illness.

"I have never been cared for when I was sick. That's one reason I decided to stop being ill. It's very inconvenient when you still have to do everything for yourself."

He was only half aware of what he was saying.

"What do you mean no one ever took care of you?"

"Just that. But then, I didn't allow anyone in my room."

"When you were a child?"

"I had to make a boundary. I had to lock her out. And I could never go out the door. I had to use the walls." He'd maybe been…seven when he'd discovered that trick. He'd felt very big then, but now in his memory the boy was so, so small.

"I think you're delirious."

Maybe. But he could remember it so well. He described it to her. "One of the bookcases turned. I kept it empty. I didn't like all those books sitting there and collecting dust anyway. I always kept the door locked. And I don't think she ever knew about the passages. If she had known about them she would've filled them up. They were my secret. And they helped me get around the house."

"You locked your mother out of your room?"

"Everyone. *Everyone.* But then, she didn't take care of me when I was sick. No one ever has. Who took care of you?"

He wanted to imagine her life. Not his. Not that little boy.

"Oh. Everyone. My grandmother. My mother. Even my dad."

"What was that like?"

Suddenly he wanted to know. He wanted to know what it was like if the people around you were… If they were normal. If they could care in a way that was normal. He just was very desperate to know.

"Well," she said. "They used to make me tea and soup.

Wipe my brow, like I've been doing for you. Keep me cool. They'd rub menthol on my chest."

He looked at her, and then down at her delicate hands. And suddenly, his feelings were much less that of a child longing to be cared for. He didn't wish her to touch him in an abstract, caring way. He wanted those hands on him in a different way.

"Are you going to rub my chest?"

Her cheeks turned pink. He supposed it was very bad form to say something like that when she was trying so hard to take care of him. But he found he couldn't help himself.

"I think you can rub your own chest," she said.

"But it sounds nicer to think of you doing it," he said.

"Are you trying to flirt with me?"

He chuckled. For some reason that was funny.

"I don't flirt."

"No?"

"No. If I want a woman I simply tell her. And then I have her."

"I see. Do they need to want you to?"

"They always do."

She moved away from him then. He wished that she hadn't.

"I'm going to come and check on you again soon. I'll just…get more water. And get more cool cloths. Hot water and cold water. Everything."

And then, when she left, he found himself drifting out of consciousness again. And dreaming of her hands.

CHAPTER SIX

SHE COULDN'T BREATHE. Being in the room with him when he didn't have a shirt on like that was… It was terrible. Because he was half-delirious, it was obvious. The stories that he had been telling about his childhood didn't make any sense. She had tried to figure out what the truth of that could possibly be, what the whole truth could be from the little bits and pieces that he had tried to tell her.

There was something in his words that was just so tortured. Whether everything he'd said was true or not, she didn't know, but it made her chest hurt.

He was just so… He was so gorgeous and masculine and feral, and she had never seen anything like him. He was like an old-fashioned movie star. Broad-chested and muscular, dark hair sprinkled over golden skin. She had wanted to rub his chest. That was just a mess. She couldn't be lusting after a man who was half out of his mind.

A man she didn't even like. Yes, it was nice that he had taken care of her while she was ill, and now he was ill probably because of her, no matter that she had tried to blame it on outside forces, but that didn't mean that she should be… Thinking about him that way.

Her grandmother would be shocked. Shocked to know that her granddaughter was alone in a house with a man, first of all, and second of all, ogling his bare chest.

She had always been so well-behaved where men were concerned.

Because you never met one that you wanted.

Well, what good did it do to want this one? He might be beautiful, but he was… Incomprehensible. He thought that caring about things, that sentimentality was a defect of some kind.

He clearly cared for nothing and no one.

And then when he had talked about women…

They always wanted him? He was so incredibly full of himself.

And yet, she could believe it. That, she didn't think was from illness delirium. That, she was afraid, was the truth of it.

That women were quite interested in him, everywhere he went, always. And that if he said that he wanted them, then… Well, then he could have them.

What would you do if he wanted you?

She shoved that aside.

He couldn't consent right now. He was half out of his mind.

She tried to busy herself in the kitchen. She made homemade soup, and thought about him saying he didn't like leftovers. He had an issue with fresh food. But then

he had said he was rich. And he had talked about locking his bedroom door and escaping through secret passages.

His story didn't line up or make sense, and she mused on that as she quickly delivered him soup.

She decided to google him. She didn't get any more information from there. In fact, she got far less. The family was wealthy, Italian, and had been in property development for nearly a century. His mother had been a brilliant businesswoman. Beautiful, too. There were pictures of her online, but only to a point. He had said that she had retreated from public life. That they hadn't left their house.

While no articles stated that directly, it was definitely implied. But there were no further details. None whatsoever.

But if she connected the dots, and filled in the blank spaces using what she knew of him—sophisticated and wild all at the same time—she had no trouble believing...

That he'd been a child left on his own. That he hadn't learned how to connect with people, not really. That he was a man who needed control because his mother had controlled so much of his life until that moment.

She sighed and pushed back away from the computer. Then she went into the kitchen, and stood there at the counter. She shouldn't want to go back upstairs so badly. She shouldn't miss him. He was her *enemy*.

Except that didn't feel like the right label, and it should.

Was she that stupid? A man was handsome so it didn't

feel right to label him the bad guy? He was the bad guy. He was a property developer who devoured adorable, unique places like Holiday House. He didn't care about her. He didn't care about what she wanted. Except he had taken care of her, even though he had no idea how to do it. And now he was lying upstairs all feverish. And handsome.

More than handsome.

She chewed on her thumbnail.

She made another cup of tea, and decided to go back upstairs. When she walked through his bedroom door, she saw him lying there on the bed, one muscular arm thrown up over his face, his body completely out of the covers, his chest bare. Every time he took a breath, the muscles on his chest and stomach shifted. She was fascinated by him. Surely there was no harm in looking, just for a moment. At the well-defined muscles, the tanned skin and dark hair that covered them. At just how very masculine he was. She had no experience of this. And she didn't wish that she did. Because it was a sort of magical thing for it to be him. Because he was so singular. So glorious.

She let out a sharp breath, and walked over to his bedside, putting the cup of tea down on the side table.

And she let herself take in all that masculine beauty. She felt outside herself in that moment, even in this very familiar room.

As she looked at every dip and hollow of muscle on his chest, his stomach.

Just looking at him made her feel…bold.

What if…

Her breathing quickened.

What if he was the first? What if he was…for her. Not forever, obviously, she wasn't that silly. But there had to be a first, didn't there? And he was definitely the only man who had ever made her feel like this.

She wanted her same life, she did.

But what if she could be different in it? Just for a while…

He shifted, lowering his arm. Sweat beaded on his forehead, and he looked… In pain. Which she hated.

She frowned, and put her hand against his face. He was burning. Without thinking, she let her hand drift down his cheek, the line of his jaw. The dark shadow of his beard was rough against her finger. He had been clean-shaven when he had arrived, but not so now.

She hadn't realized quite how fascinating men were. Quite how different.

Her admiration of them had always been distant. Mostly fictional. The problem with the men in town was that she had known them since they were boys. And they were distinctly uninteresting. It was difficult to see someone as sexy when you could so clearly remember them from middle school. Middle school was the least sexy phase of life.

And it had badly damaged the way that she saw every local guy.

It didn't seem to inhibit many of the people that

she knew from school. So many of them had married each other.

It was just that… It had never been right for her. She was very clear on that. She'd wanted to find someone who captured her imagination.

So here she was, snowed in with a mysterious, handsome stranger. No one would ever think that would happened to Noelle Holiday. No, she was staid and boring. She was a homebody. She was old before her time, basically a cat lady without cats living on top of the mountain by herself.

And she was happy with that.

Mostly.

She realized that she was still touching his face. He moved without warning. Like lightning. And suddenly, his iron grip was around her wrist. She gasped and tried to pull away, but with his eyes still closed, he yanked her toward him. "Why are you so far away?" he asked.

His breath was hot against her cheek, and her breasts were crushed to his chest. She didn't even know if he was conscious of what he was doing. Or if he was absolutely and completely delirious.

"Rocco…"

"You smell good," he said.

She shivered. He was so hot. And she knew it was because he was feverish, but this felt… It felt like more. It felt like something else. Something that it wasn't.

She couldn't let herself get carried away by this. It was a sickness. Psychotic.

But her heart was pounding wildly, and it wasn't because she was afraid.

"You should be in bed with me," he said.

And any resistance that she had access to before was gone. She felt herself melting into him, and then he shifted, and his mouth connected with hers.

She had never been kissed before.

It was so… Disruptive. She had always imagined that a kiss would be sweet. That it would be a lovely, comforting sort of thing.

She did not feel comforted.

His mouth took no prisoners, it moved over hers with expert precision. And she found herself parting her lips for him, allowing him to push his tongue between her lips and stroke it over hers.

She gasped, and that only let him take the kiss deeper.

And she wanted it.

What did that say about her? The man was in a delirium. A feverish haze, and he also was supposed to be her enemy. No matter that she couldn't seem to cement that idea in her mind.

Enemies.

But he kissed like every dream she hadn't been experienced enough to have, and she couldn't bring herself to move away from him. She let him claim her. Let each pass of his tongue make her into something new. Into someone she didn't recognize.

She wanted him. She wanted this.

He moved his hand to the back of her head, holding

her to him as he kissed her, on and on. She shivered, the sensual haze spreading from where his mouth met hers, through her limbs. She felt drugged in the most delicious way. Like she had just had a hot toddy by the fireplace, and everything in her was languid and warm.

She moved her hand down to his chest. Remembered what he had said. About wanting her to rub his chest.

She let her fingers drift over him. The prickly hair, firm muscles, hot skin...

What are you doing?

She gasped, and ripped herself away from him.

"Don't go," he said.

"You're sick," she said. "You don't even know who I am. You don't even know what you're doing."

"Sure I do," he said.

But he never opened his eyes.

"You can't consent," she said.

His eyes did drift open then, dark and furious, and connected with hers. "Excuse me?"

"You're out of your mind. You're on cold medicine, and you have a fever, and I'm taking advantage of you."

"I think you will find, *cara*, that I am more than able to consent and to act."

She shook her head, and took a step away from him, she bumped against the side table, sending the cup of tea down onto the floor, the porcelain clattering, thankfully not breaking, but the hot liquid going everywhere.

"Oh, fiddlesticks," she said. "Now look what you did. Look what I did. I... I'm sorry. I'm very sorry. I... I've never done this before, and I don't..." She picked the cup up. She would come back with a cloth. Her heart was pounding so hard, humiliation, thwarted need, and everything else, leaving her completely out cold. She went back down to the kitchen, and put her face in her hands.

She had kissed him.

Or she had let him kiss her. It wasn't entirely material, she didn't think. Which thing it was. He had a cold, a fever, and she was supposed to be taking care of him.

Does it feel better, if you make it your fault, if you make yourself feel guilty?

Tears sprang into her eyes, and she dashed them away.

Maybe it did. Maybe it felt better to make herself feel like she was some undersexed virgin who had taken advantage of a man in her care, rather than a woman who had responded to mutual attraction. No. Because that was too dangerous. The whole situation was far too dangerous.

They were working in opposition to each other. There was nothing that could be done about that. He wanted to try and manipulate this property away from her. She was refusing.

And if she showed him she was attracted to him, well...he'd undoubtedly think he could use that against her.

Her cheeks suddenly went hot. Because she worried he might actually be able to use it against her.

She was a virgin after all, and woefully inexperienced

with men and even though it had been a choice, even though she wanted to believe that she was savvy...

There were no guarantees that an actual real-life love affair wouldn't change her, just enough, that she could be manipulated in ways she couldn't foresee now.

There was no compromise to be had there.

She let out a long, slow breath. She would make dinner.

And she would hope that when he woke up he didn't remember what had happened.

CHAPTER SEVEN

ROCCO GOT OUT of bed, and grimaced when he stepped into a cold puddle.

He looked down, and saw that it looked as if there was a spilled drink there on the floor, though there was no cup. It smelled of tea. He wondered if he had knocked it over in his half delirium.

He felt better. As if the fever had broken. He looked out the window and saw that it was dark. He wondered how long he had slept.

It took him a moment to find where the clock was in the room, and the digital readout indicated that it was only six o'clock in the evening. At least, he assumed it was the evening.

He turned the light on, and found a T-shirt, shrugging it on before walking out of the bedroom. He felt driven to find Noelle, though he couldn't say why.

He paused. The memory of her hands on his face, of the way she'd cared for him stopped him cold. His chest felt sore, his body suddenly immobilized. Why was it like this?

He had never…felt sore in his heart like this thinking about a woman.

But then, no one had ever taken care of him like that before.

He was familiar enough with sexual touch. But the way she'd touched him, the way she'd soothed him, that was something else entirely.

His stomach growled, and he thought perhaps he wanted to find her because he needed food. That was reasonable enough.

He made his way down the stairs, and didn't see her. He walked into the library, and there she was, sitting in a chair by the fireplace.

"I'm hungry," he said.

She startled and turned. She was looking at him as if he had grown a second head. It was possible that he was being rude.

"I made dinner," she said.

"Thank you," he said, those words felt so foreign to him, and yet he had found himself saying them to her often.

"You're welcome," she said.

She was staring at him. He couldn't quite work out why.

"Are you well?"

"Perfectly," she said.

She stood up, and attempted what he could only describe as a scurry when she went past him. He reached out and took her arm. Forcing her to face him. Her eyes connected with his, and his gaze dropped to her mouth. And suddenly he remembered.

He had kissed her. He had pulled her down onto the bed, and he had…

He let go of her and took a step back. "I'm sorry," he said. Those words really were foreign on his lips. He never said them. He never had occasion to. He was never wrong.

But this had been wrong. He had been half out of his mind, he hadn't made sure that she even *wanted* to kiss him, he had held her to him, and then she had run away. She had spilled the tea. That was what had happened.

The touching had not been comforting, it had, in fact, been sexual and while he felt like a brute for how it must have occurred there was something placating in the realization that it was sexual, and familiar to him for that reason.

It wasn't different.

It wasn't singular.

"I was… Not thinking."

"Oh, I know," she said.

"No, I mean… I had a fever and I…"

"I know," she practically wailed. "And I feel terrible."

"You feel terrible?"

"Yes," she said. "It was wrong with me to do that. I took advantage of you."

He barked out a helpless laugh. "You took advantage of me?"

"Yes."

"You are tiny. And the first time I saw you, you were dressed as a deer. You are hardly a seductive siren. I am the one that took advantage."

"Now you're insulting me on top of everything else."

"Nothing that I said was an insult, it was simply true."

"Well, it was bracing," she said. "And not fair."

"What do you not find fair about it, little one?"

"It's... Okay. Maybe it's true. Maybe I'm not a seductive siren. But I knew what I was doing. I mean, I meant to kiss you. You didn't force me to. But you clearly wouldn't have chosen to kiss me if you weren't out of your mind."

"That is categorically untrue," he said, feeling the danger rise up inside of him. Feeling the warning. He shouldn't be saying this, he shouldn't be drawing closer to her, none of this should be happening right now.

"Well, you didn't kiss me until you had a fever, so we can't prove it, can we."

"You are a silly girl, and unless you want to find yourself flat on your back in front of that fireplace, I suggest that you stop pushing me."

Her hands had been so soft on his skin. The way that she had cared for him... No one else had ever done that. It was that caring hand on his face, that was what had undone him upstairs. That sweet way that she had touched him. It left him feeling... Not himself. It left him feeling on edge.

Because he understood attraction. But there was something else with her. Everything he had said was true. She was tiny. And she had been dressed like a reindeer. Nothing about that should appeal to him. And yet she did.

The easiest thing would be to kiss her. The easiest thing would be to reduce it to sex. Because that was what he understood. That was the connection he always had with women. The only physical touch that had ever existed in his life.

Not this…soothing of his fevered brow. Not this… wide-eyed country girl care that she was forcing upon him.

"Who says I don't want that?" she asked breathlessly, her eyes round as copper coins.

"Do not push me," he said. "I knew exactly what I was doing. I am not a nice man."

"I already know that. You're trying to take my home from me. But you also took care of me when I was unwell."

"I am a man with a strong sense of honor, but that doesn't make me nice. And it doesn't make me good. Do you know how many women I've had?"

"No. Because you didn't tell me. And the internet wasn't really forthcoming with information about you."

He lifted a brow. "You googled me?"

"Well yes. Obviously."

"There is nothing obvious about that." Or perhaps there was, and most people simply wouldn't admit to such a thing.

"There should be," she said.

She was entirely artless. And he was a brute. But he was giving her a chance. A chance to turn away from this. To turn away from him. Yes. He was giving her a chance to make a wise decision, rather than a foolish one. And if she was a fool, then it was on her head. Her…antlers.

It was not up to him to protect her from him. He was giving her ample chance. Ample choice.

"I… I want you," she said.

Her face turned scarlet.

"Why?" he asked.

"You're… A handsome, mysterious stranger. Who wouldn't want that?"

That made sense to him. And he latched onto it. He wasn't special. She wasn't romanticizing this, not beyond the sexual fantasy inherent in sleeping with someone that you ought not to.

He wanted her, because he wanted this to make sense. And it did make sense. They were a man and woman snowed in together, so why shouldn't they?

She wasn't special. This was biology. He was not special to her. He was simply an object of desire.

He could understand that.

It pleased him.

He moved closer to her, and gripped her chin, tilting her face up and forcing her eyes to meet his. "That's what you want, then? The fantasy. Snowed in here at the top of this mountain? Does your snowplow actually work?"

She huffed a laugh. "I wish that I was that crafty, but

I'm not. We really are stuck here. It's really… All of this, but my life is very unexciting. This is the most exciting thing that's ever happened. And I…" She looked up at him. "Am I worthy of a little bit of excitement?"

"You are worthy of being worshiped," he said. "Let me show you."

He dipped his head and kissed her lips. They were softer than he remembered. She was soft. He pulled her against him, moving his hands over her curves, bringing her flush against him. He held her tightly.

She was glorious. Everything he had ever fantasized about and more.

It was just sex.

What a relief.

Because he understood this. Because this made sense. And he could have her. He could have this.

He kissed her, deep and long and endlessly.

He kissed her because he wanted her.

He kissed her until she was whimpering, until she brought her hands up to grip the fabric of his T-shirt. She was kneading him like a little cat, her nails sharp through the fabric.

"You do want me," he said, looking down at her.

She turned red again. "Yes," she said. "Sorry."

"Don't apologize for your passion. You're beautiful."

He was going to show her. He was going to show her exactly what he wanted to do with her. Petite and pretty and about to be his.

The snow would melt. He would buy this place, and

he would level it. They would never see each other again. She would hate him after.

But she wanted him now. So he would have her.

It was that simple.

This was simple.

It would change nothing. Because nothing ever changed him.

He picked her up, and carried her over to the fireplace, laying her down on the plush rug. A kick of annoyance hit him in the chest. He didn't think he had any condoms with him. This was a business trip, and he was one to keep things compartmentalized. He thought it was perhaps a little bit too much to ask that the woman who had been dressed like a deer had condoms.

"I don't have protection," he said.

She looked confused for a moment. "Oh," she said. She frowned deeply. "I take birth control."

He was fastidious in all things, and he knew that he had nothing to worry about as far as cleanliness. Perhaps she made a habit of sleeping with men when she didn't have condoms. He doubted it.

"If that's all right with you," he said.

She nodded. "It is. It's okay with me."

The color in her cheeks was high, but it wasn't from embarrassment now. She seemed excited.

"Good. Now that we have gotten responsibility out of the way."

He stripped his shirt off, and the rest of his clothes. Her shoulders were scrunched up by her ears, and it looked as if she wasn't certain where she was allowed to look.

"What?" he asked.

"You just… Oh… You are… Impressive."

There was something so sweet, so guileless about the way that she said that. About the way that she looked at him. He couldn't help but be charmed. He couldn't help but be mesmerized.

"It's your turn now."

He knelt down beside her, and stripped her sweater off. The bra she was wearing was simple, pretty. White with a little bow in the center. Definitely not the kind of underwear he was used to seeing on a woman. This wasn't for show. But for practicality. He found himself transfixed.

"I'm not… I mean my boobs aren't very big," she said.

"They're perfect," he said, the understatement of the century. He unclipped her bra, and pulled it off, revealing small, perfectly formed breasts. The tips were rosy pink and beautiful.

His breath hissed through his teeth, tension gathering in his chest. "More than fine. You are beautiful," he said.

He leaned forward, and kissed the sweet curve of her neck, down to her breasts, taking one crest into his mouth and sucking hard. She arched against him, a rough sound in her throat.

And he found that he was driven for her to make that sound as many times as possible.

Yes. He was.

He hooked his finger in the waistband of her leggings, and her underwear, and dragged them down her body, leaving her bare for his appraisal.

He kissed his way down her stomach, down to the sweet center between her thighs, where he began to taste her.

She gasped, and he thought she even tried to pull away from him, but he didn't allow it.

"Let me pleasure you," he said.

He nuzzled her there, parting her legs for him as he began to lick toward her center.

"Rocco," she said, her fingers pushed into his hair.

Yes.

She arched against him, saying his name over and over again like a prayer.

Her hands moved through his hair. It reminded him of the way that she had touched him when she was caring for him while he was ill.

Maybe he was still sick. He felt dizzy. Dizzy with need for her. With the flavor of her coating his tongue. She was like a drug, one that he was more than happy to indulge in.

He pleasured her like that until he felt her body draw up tight like a bow. Then he pushed one finger inside of her, continuing to lick her as he did. And he felt her shatter. She gasped, crying out his name, forking her fingers through his hair and rolling her hips against him.

He growled, surging up her body and claiming her mouth with his, swallowing her cries of pleasure.

Then he positioned himself between her thighs, and thrust home.

She was tight. So tight.

And the way that she cried out didn't feel like pleasure now, but pain.

He looked down at her face.

"Noelle?"

"Don't stop," she said, arching against him. And he was powerless to deny her. He began to move, thrusting deep and hard. Until she began to relax, until she became pliant against him. He moved against her, again and again.

He wanted to take her to the peak one last time. He couldn't please only himself.

He moved his hand between them, began to rub her with his thumb, and she dug her fingers into his shoulder, crying out as she pulsed around him, and then he lost control. He thrust into her once, twice, surging inside of her, his orgasm overtaking him like a train.

He poured his desire out inside of her, kissed her lips, let her swallow his roar of need.

And they lay there like that, sweat-slicked. He was undone.

"You were a virgin," he said.

It didn't seem possible, and yet it did. She was the strangest woman that he had ever met. The only person that he had ever met who was as isolated as he was.

He let that realization rest heavy on his shoulders. He wasn't a virgin. He had traveled the world. And many women had touched his body. But no one had touched him deeper than that.

Her life was different. She was in this small town, where anyone you slept with, you would have to contend with again. He imagined it changed the complexion of how people did things.

Perhaps.

"Noelle…"

"Okay," she said, sounding grumpy. "I was. But… I don't expect anything from you."

She looked sad, though. And the trouble was, he now expected something. The trouble was, something had changed. This place, it didn't mean anything to him, not specifically, and it did to her.

Which was beginning to matter. She was not just a faceless person he could fling money at. Was not just a number or a statistic. She was a woman. Who had taken care of him.

Sex was one thing. It was everything else.

But he was caught. Caught in the web of his mother's making. In her game.

He had wanted to dodge it. He had thought that he could serve his own ambitions while completing the terms of the will, and it would never bother him. But it bothered him now.

There was only one other way to sidestep it.

He would have to think about this. Not what he was going to do. He was determined on that. But how he was going to do it.

Rocco Moretti had yet to enter into a battle that he hadn't won. But he had a feeling if anyone was going to challenge him in ways that he couldn't anticipate, it was her.

She had been pushing him from the moment they'd met. Refusing to give in to offers of money, caring for him even when she claimed not to like him.

But he would be able to win. He knew it.

Just then, the phone rang.

"Oh," she said, scrambling up. It was the landline.

"You have an actual phone?" he asked.

"This is a bed-and-breakfast," she said. She was naked, shivering, she didn't quite know what to do with herself, but she gathered herself to answer the phone.

"Holiday House."

"Is that you, Noelle?"

"Yes," she said.

"This is Fred, we're headed up to plow your road."

"Oh," she said. "Thank God."

"Everything should be open for you within the hour."

"Thank you," she said.

She hung up the phone. And suddenly she felt bereft. They were free now. They had… Cared for each other while they were sick. She had just lost her virginity.

And the roads would be open.

He could leave. She was suddenly seized with the strangest sense of grief. It didn't make any sense. She shouldn't be grieving.

She had known that this would happen. It was okay that it was happening.

Still, she felt overcome.

"I… The road is going to be cleared today," she said.

"Oh," he said. "Then we can go to town."

"Yes," she said. "You can leave—what?"

"We can go to town," he said. "Noelle, I want to see this town. The way that you do."

It was the nicest, most unexpected thing he could've said.

"Okay," she said.

That was how she found herself bundled up two hours later, and headed down to town with Rocco. She hadn't really thought this through. She felt raw from having made love to him. She felt overawed by him in the entire situation, in fact.

And she was going to town, where she would run into people that she undoubtedly knew, and she would be forced to look at them in the eye and not announce that she had just had sex with this man.

This man who was now going to leave.

She ignored the lancing pain in her heart.

She had bigger problems on her hands. He was still going to try to take the bed-and-breakfast away from her.

That was a much bigger problem than him leaving. She felt torn in half, and she didn't want to examine it.

What if she'd played right into his hand? She was more afraid of the sex being an act of manipulation than she was of actually being manipulated by it.

Which maybe didn't make sense, but she wasn't sure she was thinking clearly.

He parked his car on the street, and he surprised her by taking her hand when they began to walk down the sidewalk.

"People know me here," she said.

"And? Do you have an attachment to them seeing you as Mother Mary?"

"No," she said. "I don't have an attachment to that at all."

"Well, that is good. Because you are decidedly no longer virginal."

"But people will talk," she said.

"And you care about that?"

She thought about it. No. Not really. But she was predictable. She'd always been Noelle Holiday of Holiday House and she'd never dated any men around town. So no one…thought of her like that really.

So nobody would see this coming. And they wouldn't be able to figure out what exactly it meant. She liked that.

Why not? Why not revel in walking down the street with the most handsome man she had ever seen.

So she did. From shop to shop. She took him to the ice skating rink that was put over the top of the parking lot every year in the center of town. They didn't skate, but they watched people. She took him to the town Christmas tree, and through any number of shops that boasted the best souvenirs in town. He declined to buy any. Not even the taxidermist raccoon holding a banjo. Which, if she were a billionaire, she probably would have bought. Because it was hilarious.

Everywhere they went, people said hi to her. And to him. They looked at them with curiosity, and she simply smiled.

Then they went into Sweet Melody, and she walked to the counter with him smiling, and ordered them both hot chocolate.

"Hi, Noelle," Melody said, her eyebrows rising up to her hairline.

"Hello," she said cheerfully.

"Who is this?"

"Melody Stevens, this is Rocco Moretti. We got snowed in up at the inn," she said.

"Oh," Melody said.

Noelle smiled cheerfully.

"We need to go out to dinner soon," she said.

"Oh, we will," Noelle said.

She walked back out of the coffeehouse holding Rocco's hand still, and drinking the hot chocolate. He grimaced as he said, "It's very sweet."

"Yes," she said. "It is."

They looked around, she wondered if maybe, just maybe, him having an attachment to the town would change the way that he saw Holiday House. If it would change his intentions.

"So," she said. "What do you think?"

"I hate it."

He took another sip of hot chocolate.

She simply stared at him. "You… You hate it?"

"Yes. Everyone knows you…they talk to you constantly. It is saccharine to the point of being sickening, and I am not talking about the hot chocolate. The decorations are too bright, and it is too much. But you clearly love it."

"I do," she said.

"You love it, and you would do anything to preserve your life here, yes?"

"Yes."

Her heart was pounding, she didn't know where this was going.

"I have something to ask you."

"Okay."

He looked around the street, and the Christmas lights reflected in his dark eyes. Then he looked back at her, and they were nothing but coal black. "Noelle Holiday, I want you to be my wife."

CHAPTER EIGHT

NOELLE WAS SHOCKED. Immobilized. Of all the things she'd expected from her first sexual experience—which had been amazing but clearly, clearly a one-off—a proposal hadn't been on the list.

She might have been only just recently a virgin, but she wasn't an idiot.

"Excuse me?"

She was so aware that she was standing out there on the streets of this town where everybody knew her. Where everyone had opinions on who she was, with this man. And it had been an extremely fun lark, until this moment. Until she had begun to realize that whatever she thought was happening, Rocco knew better. Until she had begun to realize that he never just did anything. This had been a calculated, coordinated move. He wasn't going to look at the town with her simply because he wanted to. No. Of course not. There was something else at play with him. She had forgotten for a moment who he was. Even though she had been telling herself to be conscious of it. To be aware.

"Why?" she asked.

Not the response she ever saw herself giving to a man in her fantasies when he proposed. But then, the man had never been Rocco.

She couldn't have conjured him up in her fantasies no matter how hard she tried.

"Because. I either have to continue building, forever and ever, or I have to marry and produce an heir. You don't want me to build over the top of Holiday House. Increasingly, I don't want that either."

"Why not?" she asked.

"Because it would hurt you," he said. "And I don't want to do that."

She clung to that. Imagined holding it in her fist like a bright, shiny jewel.

If he cared about hurting her did that mean he cared?

Or was this the manipulation?

She didn't know, but she knew what she wanted to believe.

"But… But what would marriage between us entail?"

"I think we only just had a small sample of what it entails," he said, his voice low and seductive, and how she hated him for that. How she hated him for the ease with which he could take her back there. Could make her want to say yes regardless of whether or not it made any sense.

That bastard.

Was this what he had always planned on doing?

"You are looking at me as if I am a monster, and you did not look at me like that only moments ago," he said.

Her face went all hot and she resented it.

"You… Is that why you slept with me?" She was so aware that she knew the people who were passing by, at least by face, if not by name. So aware that she was playing out this intimate moment for all the town to see.

"No," he said. "Of course not. Of course that is not why."

"Was it your plan all along?"

"No. My plan was to bulldoze your bed-and-breakfast and build a hugely lucrative resort property. But this is another way forward. An alternative."

"What if I don't want your alternative?"

"Then I will proceed as I had originally planned. That is up to you. Though I do not know why you would want to make it so difficult."

She realized then that she was standing at the cusp of an improbable issue. An unsolvable problem. She couldn't go back to the life that she had known before he had come into it. That was the simple truth. She had been trying so hard to cling to her existence. To what she knew. And part of her had believed that once he left, as long as she won, as long as she was able to win this fight with him, then she would be able to go back to the way things had been. To that simpler time. Her simpler self.

But it wasn't true.

She was changed by knowing him.

It was an utterly horrendous thing to realize. She was altered for having met the man. Part of her would always be missing if he was gone from her.

No, she wasn't in love with him, but she felt something

for him. There was no pretending that she didn't. And if he left, if he went away, it wouldn't be like he had never come there. Because she could never be untouched by him. Unkissed by him. She could never go back to how it had been before she was possessed by him. She was changed. Forevermore.

And always she would be living a half life. The one from before and the one after.

"So wait a minute," she said. "I marry you and…"

"I will give your mother the money that she wants. She will be cared for. The mother-in-law of a billionaire. You will have Holiday House, preserved, though you will not be able to be there all the time, you will of course be able to go there as you wish."

"But you and I will be married."

"Yes. And I live mostly in New York City."

She grimaced. "New York City. I have never been there, but it sounds vile."

He chuckled. "Most people are enamored of it. It is the greatest city in the world, after all."

"Subjective, I'm certain. Also, I love it here. I love it here more than I love anything else."

"How nice for you," he said. "I think you will find that isn't true for others. I for example, find that I am not so charmed by this place."

"No, of course not. That would be far too convenient. Can't you just fall in love with this place and decide not to build here out of the goodness of your heart?"

He shook his head. "I don't do anything out of the

goodness of my heart. But the truth is, eventually, I will have to marry, and I will have to have an heir. You took care of me. When I was ill. You made me feel at ease. You are exactly the woman that I should want as the mother to my child. Yes, I find your house not to my taste, but it is homey. I think. At least, I suppose that is what others would say."

"But not you."

"I find it cluttered. But it is not dangerously so."

She didn't have any idea what he meant by that. By dangerously cluttered. What on earth could that mean?

"I think that you would be a good mother. I think that you could learn to be a good wife. We are compatible in bed."

She looked around, wildly. "I know everyone here."

"I don't. But in any case, you and I would suit."

"How? I hate the sound of the place that you call home, you hate the place that I call home. You think my house is cluttered. You think that I'm a silly small-town girl."

"You were also a virgin," he said, lowering his voice. "I take the gift that you gave me seriously."

"You make it sound like it's medieval times. Should I be grateful you didn't hang the bloodied sheet out the window?"

He frowned. "Did you bleed?"

"If so, not enough to worry about."

"I don't want to have hurt you."

"I'm a woman, Rocco, if I got wound up about a little blood I'd be beset all the time."

He considered that. "I don't mean to sound medieval. But perhaps a bit old-fashioned. I cannot help myself. I cannot ignore the fact that you have never been with another man, and yet you chose to be with me. There are things I cannot give, Noelle. I will be honest with you in that. I cannot give love. I will not give you a conventional life. I do not think that we will sit warmly around the dinner table all together, and talk of our day. I will come and see you, and the child. You will stay with me sometimes. You will be… The better parent, I feel, in the child's life."

"I didn't even tell you if I wanted children," she said, even as she felt her stomach cramp low. The idea of carrying a baby… Of course she had always wanted a traditional life. It was the thing that she thought about often. Her family home, her family legacy. In order to truly realize that dream, she had seen herself having her own family. She had also seen herself living with that family at Holiday House. She hadn't considered being a part-time single mother.

But she couldn't go back to that simple dream. Because she could no longer put a blank face in the place of the father, the husband. The only man that she could imagine was Rocco. And she didn't have to be in love with him for that to be the case. She wasn't in love. She wasn't that naive, she wasn't that simple. But she also knew that attraction like they shared didn't just pop up all the time. In twenty-four years, she hadn't experienced it. Now that she knew it existed, she could never settle for less. Was she going to wait another twenty-four years for a man to show up who ignited her imagination in that way?

She thought of her mother, her father, who had clearly been incompatible in the end. They had loved each other. They truly had. But her mother had wanted to escape the life that they had built, whatever she had thought going into it. What that taught her was that you couldn't know for certain what you would want in the future. You could only make decisions as best you could right then.

It was all you could do.

It was the only thing.

She might be unhappy if she decided to marry him. But she would be unhappy if she didn't. She would still be in this fight. This fight to keep Holiday House, this fight to... To find herself. Because in the end, that's what she was trying to do. She had tried to do it by keeping everything the same. She had been lonely. Happy in so many ways, how she loved the Christmas tree farm. How she loved the house. How she loved the people in this town. But she was unsatisfied. She was unfulfilled. Maybe she could be half and half. The before and the after. Noelle, with her child, with her warmth and her Christmas, at Holiday House, and Rocco's wife in New York when he needed it.

Yes, what he was offering had a bleakness to it. But,

she was happy with him now. She had been these past few days. He was a good man.

He would continue to be a good man. Who was to say that it wouldn't be enough?

Who could know for certain?

"I will marry you. But I need it in writing that Holiday House will be safe."

"It will."

"What will become of the other properties that you bought?"

"A preserve. For the local wildlife, and for the town."

She couldn't help herself. She threw her arms around him. "Rocco, that is amazing. The most beautiful gift that you could've given."

"You're very welcome," he said, his voice turning to stone. "Then we have ourselves a bargain."

"Yes."

"How long will it take for you to secure staff that can manage in your stead?"

"I do have staff. But…"

"Then it will work out. If I need to call someone in from one of my hotels to help manage, then I shall."

"I have a feeling they will feel that that is entirely beneath them."

"But I'm their boss, so they shall do as I ask."

"Oh."

She felt right then that she hadn't exactly understood what she was saying yes to. Because she knew the man in context of her life, she knew him in black-and-white on a Google search. But she didn't fully understand the place that he occupied in the world. How could she? How could she.

"We must leave as soon as possible," he said. "I have to announce my engagement so I can put a stop to my mother's expansion stipulations."

Her whole life was changing, and she could barely catch her breath.

But she realized it didn't matter.

Because she was prepared to follow him, breathless.

So perhaps his manipulation had worked.

She wasn't even sure she cared if that were true.

Rocco did not tarry. He called his people in as quickly as they could arrive and had them help pack Noelle's necessities. He asked that they outfit the plane with clothing and makeup suitable for his bride. She was cute in her normal attire, but cute would not be fitting for a Moretti bride.

Then she was bundled up and loaded onto his private plane, as he did his best to make sure that everything at the bed-and-breakfast and Christmas tree farm was secured to Noelle's specifications.

As they stood there in the doorway of Holiday House, all her things being put in the car caravan so that they could make the journey to New York with them, he palmed the jewelry box in his pocket. He had his assistant whisk the finest diamond she could get her hands on immediately to him. Because he would have this secured as soon as possible.

He held the box out, and opened it. "Here. Until we can sign a contract, this is my promise to you. There are expectations that come with it."

She was looking at the ring, boggling.

"Expectations?"

"When we get off the plane there will doubtless be paparazzi there. You must expect it. By now, the world knows that I have been snowed in at the top of a mountain. And I prefer to make the most of the story. I am considered a ruthless, heartless property developer."

"Yes. I have some experience with that."

"So you have. But this will change the story. Do you not understand all the ways in which you are perfect for this position?"

"You make it sound like a job."

"In many ways it is. For my wife, being married to me was always going to be a job. Not only will there be media attention it is…possible that the board of my company will be unhappy with the development."

"Why?" she asked.

"Eternal expansion suits them, of course."

"Right."

"I was content to continue putting marriage off. I am only thirty."

"Ah right, and sperm is everlasting. You could put it off until you were eighty."

He laughed. "I never had the inclination to do that.

But I have been caught between two things all this time. The desire to be free from this excessive expansion my mother has commanded, and the desire to not yet marry. Neither option truly exists. But only when I met you did I see marriage as the more… Peaceful option. Why shouldn't I be a father? I would, after all, do better at it than my own mother. My own father being nonexistent, it would be impossible to do worse."

"Well, I don't think that's true. I think sometimes presence can be worse than absence. Depending precisely on how the presence manifests itself."

"Indeed." He thought of his mother again. Of the darkness of the house. The fetid smell. Of how she loved her things more than she had ever loved him. She could name the price of each one of them, where they had come from, the date they had been bought. She never even remembered his birthday.

"Will you wear my ring?"

She looked at him. "This ring exists so that you have a good story to tell. So that when your picture is taken as we get off the plane people will know that you fell in love with the innkeeper you were trapped on the mountain with."

"Yes. That is exactly why it exists."

She looked around. "I think this is the kind of thing I might've thought was romantic under different circumstances. I mean, if you had gotten down on one knee, and my family was here. If my dad wasn't gone. Oh, yeah, if we were in love."

She looked wounded, and what he didn't want was for her to have second thoughts, because now that he was set on this plan, he was convinced that it was the best way forward. No question.

He didn't want to continue on the way he had been. It felt like a life continually out of his control whereas...

One with her felt like it might, perhaps, be a path to a life that was much more his own.

Both were his mother's grand design, and he could not readily articulate why one felt better than the other.

Perhaps, it was Noelle.

"Would you like me to get down on one knee?"

"No. I don't need you to do that. Thanks, though. That's..."

He could see that he was losing her. He could see that she was afraid. That she was questioning things. He knew what connection they had. Where it was strongest. He cupped the back of her head and leaned down, claiming her mouth. He kissed her, deep and long until he lost himself entirely. Until he couldn't remember what he had been trying to do. Until there was nothing but her. Her softness. His need for her. Her lips, her sighs. Everything.

He was consumed by it, just as much as she was. He was caught in his own trap. It was a hell of a thing. It was unlike anything he had ever experienced before.

He did not know if he wished to drown in it, or turn away from it, never to touch it again. When he moved away from her, her eyes were still closed. She was breathing hard. So was he.

"It is not all a story," he said. "It is not all terribly unromantic."

Her eyes fluttered open.

"Yes," she said.

She put her hand out, and he took the ring carefully from the box, sliding it onto her finger. It glittered there. A promise of something.

And it was one of the few times he could honestly say that the addition of something made it better, and not simply more cluttered. Not worse.

On her, the ring was beautiful.

"Let's go," he said, gesturing toward the car.

"Okay," she said, turning to look back at the bed-and-breakfast.

"You will be back," he said.

"I know," she said.

"You look as if I'm dragging you away forever."

"You're certainly dragging me into the unknown."

"Didn't I already do that?"

Her cheeks went pink. "You can't make everything about sex."

"And why not? Sex is what brought us here. It is not a bad thing. It is our connection. It is certainly real."

"Yes," she said softly. "It is."

She was silent on the car ride to the airfield, and when they boarded the private plane, her eyes went round. "I...

I had no idea that a private plane was this luxurious. But I've only flown one time."

"Really?"

"Yes. To visit my aunt in Ohio. I was a kid. I don't even really remember it. But I... This is incredible."

"It is a necessity," he said.

He didn't feel entirely comfortable with her all over the plane, and he wasn't sure why. He was used to being around people who were blasé about wealth and luxury. Even if they were impressed they would never venture to behave as if they were. The disparity between the two of them was all the clearer here.

"It is yours now," he said. "What I mean is, everything that is mine is now yours."

"It... It is?"

"Yes," he said. "It is. We are sharing our wealth."

For some reason, that made him feel better.

"I... Good," she said. "I... I don't need wealth really. But it makes me feel better to know that you see me as a partner, and not simply an acquisition."

He didn't argue with her. He probably should. She wasn't exactly the same as an object, but she was primarily one. A wife that he'd needed to acquire in order to fulfill certain terms.

And yet, within that, she mattered.

Of course she did. It couldn't have been anyone, or he would've married already.

She was...everything he should not want, and yet

he did want her. How could he let go of such a glorious mystery?

All his life he'd felt isolated. She made him feel something more.

He did not want to let that go.

"You got awfully quiet," she said.

"Do not concern yourself with my silence," he said, settling into one of the plush leather chairs on the plane, and inviting her to do the same. His stewardess bustled about the cabin, bringing them both drinks.

"Champagne?" she asked.

"Yes," he said. "To celebrate."

"Oh," she said, looking at her hand.

She looked back up at the stewardess and smiled. "Of course."

The stewardess beamed back, and then left the two of them alone.

"My staff sign ironclad NDAs," he said. "You have no need to put on a show in front of Elise."

"Well, I feel uncomfortable," she said. "Lying."

"It isn't a lie. I came to your bed-and-breakfast, we were snowed in. We were overcome by our attraction to one another."

"Were you?"

She was staring at him, with the intense copper eyes that he found so attractive, generally speaking, but a bit off-putting now.

"Yes," he said.

He felt pinned to the spot, but he also didn't see the

use in denying it. "What is it you need to hear, Noelle? That I was attracted to you in a way that felt uncommon? In a way that tested me, and I failed that test?"

"What test?"

"It felt entirely ungentlemanly of me to claim you like I did when we were trapped in the way that we were. And yet I did, because I could not resist you. Because you were… Everything that I wanted and more. Because you are the most beautiful woman that I have ever seen. It doesn't even matter if that is strictly true in a measurable sense. You are the only one that I can remember. And I could not imagine not taking this opportunity to secure a wife when I found one who would suit me so well. You see how it is?"

"I… I suppose so."

"Is that what you wanted to hear? That you are special?"

"Not if you're only telling me that so that I'll shut up."

"I am not," he said.

He realized that this was the longest he had ever spoken to another person about something other than business in a very long time. But then, that was true of this whole lost weekend with her. She wanted to understand the way in which she was different? He couldn't begin to list a single way that she was the same.

"You have experiences that I don't have," she said. "It makes me feel… I wonder what you see in me, I guess. Is this obligation because you were my first or…"

"No. What I see in you is the ability to be a warm

and caring mother. But also… I want you." He met her gaze. "I have never cared much about a specific woman. I have cared for my own pleasure. I seek out women who are the same. So that I do not have to think about them. They think of themselves. I think of myself. I have never been… Warm. You make me feel warm."

He didn't know if what he had said made any sense at all; he wasn't even certain why he'd said it.

"My whole childhood felt magical," she said. "Holiday House is the most wonderful place to grow up. I loved it so much. I always have. I imagined growing up there. Growing old there. Raising children there. I don't know where I thought I was going to meet a man. The boys that I knew in town never impressed me. Not because I'm a snob just because… Well. Maybe I am a snob. I never wanted them. I could never quite explain why. But I didn't. Still, I imagined a warm and happy life there. When my father died, and my mother left, I suddenly realized that the life that I thought was happening around me wasn't. My mother didn't love the bed-and-breakfast. She felt trapped there. Their relationship wasn't everything that I had believed it to be, and it made me realize for the first time that a fantasy, a dream that you have when you're a child, doesn't mean anything. It isn't guaranteed to come true. So I've been up there, clinging to that place, feeling more and more lonely. Wishing for a life I didn't have anymore. Wishing for the confidence that I used to have that my life was going to turn out okay. You disrupted everything."

"You do not find me warm?"

"I find you terrifying. The prospect of something that I never once imagined, but it seems like I would be a fool to say no. Not because you're a billionaire. Because it saves Holiday House. And because… I want you. That has to matter for something."

"Certainly."

"You said some things… When you were feverish. About your childhood."

"What things?"

"They probably didn't mean anything. You were probably completely out of your mind." She frowned. "Except you did remember kissing me. And I thought you might not."

"Tell me."

"You talked about traveling through a secret passageway. And always being in your room."

"That is true," he said. His chest felt icy, and he didn't like it. Because what he wanted was to forget his childhood had ever happened. That was what he wanted.

And yet… She had shared something of herself. And he had already shared something of himself, even if he had done so when he hadn't meant to. Eventually, they would have to speak of it, because they were going to have to share a house and he was going to have to explain some of his eccentricities.

He had never considered that. What it actually meant to have to share space with another person.

Even while they had packed up all the things that she

possessed to come to his penthouse in New York City, he hadn't fully thought all that through. He had imagined tucking her up in a space in the house, rather than integrating her. But then... Wasn't he simply treating her like his mother, only in the reverse?

"As you know, my mother reached a point where she could no longer leave the house."

"You did mention that, yes."

"There was nothing that could be done about it. She was a complete and total shut-in. Her phobias took over. She began to seek ways that she could control her surroundings. The way that she found peace..." He gritted his teeth. It was difficult for him to try and justify what his mother had done when he was so angry. And yet, he had done a fair amount of work to try and assign meaning to all that she had done. For his own peace, as well as her memory. Still there were times when all he wanted to do was rage.

This was one of those times.

Because having to expose it all again. To speak to somebody about it. To admit the truth to Noelle felt exposing, even if it shouldn't. Both of the conditions that he had lived in as a child, and of his mother. And as much as he often resented his mother and her memory, he still loathed exposing her. It went against his own need to also protect. Still, he did his best. "She began to collect things. Small things at first, but it grew. And the issue with something like that, when it becomes a compulsion, when it weaves together with all the other existing phobias is that it quickly takes over every part of your life. Every room of the house."

She was staring at him. "You said... You sometimes ate expired food."

"She would hoard food as well. There was no way of knowing, often, how old something was. And she did not like to throw it out. The two members of staff that she had enabled her. I don't know if they became used to the surroundings, or if it didn't matter to them because they knew that my mother would remember them in her will, and they would be paid handsomely for the trouble of living in squalor. But for whatever reason, they acted as if everything was fine. But I couldn't. I stayed in my room as much as possible, I locked my mother out. I would not allow it to become a dumping ground for her things. I could not allow it. The only measure of peace that I had in that house was my own space. And that is why when I left I would go through the secret passages."

"You... You were so isolated," she said. "When you said that you grew up in a wealthy family, that is by far not what I imagined."

"It is not what anyone imagines. But mental illness doesn't care if you have money. She could've had access to treatment, yes, but she didn't take advantage of that access. She didn't want to be fixed. She didn't want to be better. Perhaps she couldn't have been. Perhaps it was impossible for her to be better than she was, I will never know. What I know is she lived her last years in darkness, and isolation, and in secret. And then she wanted me to continue on in her quest to hoard things. In this case, property. And I have done so, because it has grown the business, but you can see, I hate this. This empty acquisition. This need to own. I keep very little in my home, you will find."

"Oh," she said.

"I like there to be space."

"It makes sense. All the… You're quite particular."

"Now that I can control my surroundings, I do so." He could hear himself. He could hear himself talking about control, and he could even recognize that was a close neighbor of his mother's issues. But he did not think it was wrong. He did not think that he was wrong. Not truly. What he did, he did as a matter of his own survival. His own mental clarity. He liked to feel as far removed from his childhood as possible.

"I thought my childhood was perfect," she said softly. "But, my mother ran away from it all as soon as she could. I thought that she loved our life. I thought that she loved me. But the truth is, if anything, she loved my dad. As soon as he was gone, so was she. And I know it's not what you went through. But it's just funny to me, how I'm clinging to my childhood as best I can, to the memory of what I thought it was. Trying to prove that it was perfect. And you're running as far away from yours as possible."

It was two different things. The opposite things, even, and yet there was something in the sadness in her voice that made him feel like they were connected by an invisible string. He wasn't sure that he liked the sensation, but there it was. Powerful. Intense.

"And yet here you are, in the midst of change," he said, and he wasn't sure if he was pointing it out to put distance between them or simply to see what she would do. She looked down. "I made my choice."

"You must admit, I steered you quite strongly."

She nodded. "You did. You also underestimate my ability to fight, Rocco. I am strong and stubborn."

"In my experience you are not so hard to persuade."

She shook her head. "I have been opposing my mother on the sale of that house for two years now. I am very hard to persuade. I live up there, in perfect happiness with my own company. You… Changed something in me. You made me see that something else could exist. I didn't quite understand what that might look like. I still don't. But I'm here."

"You should go and get changed," he said.

"My suitcases…"

"No. In the bedroom there is some clothing for you. You will have your picture taken when you get off the plane."

"And I have to look a certain way."

"Yes."

"Like I belong with you."

He paused for a moment. "You are in the midst of change, as I only just pointed out. I think it is only fair for me to acknowledge that you are the one that will have to change the most. I am bringing you into my life. You will accompany me to different events as and when I need you to. You will get off this plane and create the photo op that I want you to create. You will have my child."

"Presumably the child will also be mine."

"Yes. I have no desire, nor the inclination or ability to be a full-time father. But these things… These changes, you're making for me. I am not changing. I feel that must be abundantly clear."

"Rocco, if you think that you can get married, bring a woman into your home, bring a child into your home and experience no change at all, I'm not sure you're living in reality. I think it's only fair to point that out to you." She stood up and stretched. "Now. I guess I'll go change." She laughed. "I only meant my clothes. But I suppose in reality it means… Everything."

CHAPTER NINE

SHE WAS LIKE a different person. Polished from head to toe. She had spent far too long of the flight on her makeup and hair. The clothes that had been provided for her were beautiful, she couldn't deny that.

But she felt a strange distance between herself and Rocco, because he had decided to put it there with his cold words about their arrangement. He had done that to them. And he had done it on purpose, she knew that. It was tempting to try and make it so he didn't win. But perhaps he was going to win just for a little bit. When she emerged from the bedroom, there was a strange light in his eyes, and she couldn't read it. She decided she wasn't going to bother.

The ring felt heavy on her hand, and the plane began to descend, which unnerved her, so she sat down and buckled her seatbelt.

Then, she took a look out the window. She could see the city off in the distance. A skyline that she had seen in movies countless times over, but had never imagined that she would see in person. She wasn't sure she had even wanted to. It was such a strange, surreal feeling.

Before she knew it, the plane's wheels connected to the ground, and they taxied for a brief moment before they came to a stop.

"A car will drive up to the door to meet us."

She looked up at him. "I imagine this is quite a different experience to typical plane travel. I only vaguely remember."

"Yes, normally you must fight through the crowd like you're in a herd of cattle."

"So you've been told?"

"Yes. I've heard."

Her heart gave a little jump start. Because maybe they were back to being them. Such as they were. Maybe there was a little bit of a connection there still. Even though he was being difficult.

The door to the plane opened smoothly, and he took her hand. She couldn't keep any physical distance between them, he was making sure of that, and when the physical distance was erased, she found that it was harder and harder to maintain emotional distance. That was the danger of him. The physical connection was just so intense.

She was startled by the first flash of the camera when they got off the plane, by the crush of people who surrounded their car. He did not seem bothered by it at all. The click and pop of each picture felt like getting hit with a tiny boulder, and she started each time. But they made their way quickly to the car, the door shutting behind them. The windows tinted, hopefully enough to conceal them from view. She didn't know if she had done what he needed her to do.

"I'm sorry," she said. "I forgot to gaze adoringly at you."

"That's quite all right. It's all right if you look surprised, because you are definitely being positioned as my sweet small-town fiancée."

She frowned. "Shouldn't there have been security keeping them away from us?"

"Yes. If I wanted that. But what I wanted was photographs. I will not be making grand explanations about where I have been spending my time these past days. Nor will I be making an announcement or telling a story about how the two of us got together. The media will fill it all in as long as we make ourselves available. They will create the narrative. If we tried to make the narrative, then it would be questioned. The public likes to make a story for themselves."

"Oh," she said.

She didn't know how she felt that her naivety was being used against her. That he liked that she had been surprised by all of that because it would make her... Well, look like what she was, she supposed. Maybe it was a manipulation so much as a calculated lack of preparation.

He was so irritating.

But then, she was captivated by the cityscape, and forgot to be irritated with him as she gazed up at the impossibly tall buildings as they wound their way slowly through the manic streets. She had never seen anything like it. The sidewalks were filled with people, the road gridlocked with cars. The sky was nearly blotted out by those buildings. So tall that when she looked up out the window she couldn't see past the end of them.

They pulled up to a building that was all black glass and steel, and the car stopped. The door was opened for them, and Rocco got out, reaching inside and taking her hand, guiding her up out of the car and onto the sidewalk, where they were met by more photographers. He wrapped his arm around her waist, and instinctively, she raised her left hand to cover her face as they walked by the photographers. Once they were inside the building he looked at her and smiled. "You showed them your ring."

She looked down at her hand. "Not intentionally. I was just… Shielding myself instinctively."

"Well, your instincts are very good."

There was no one in the black foyer of the building, and she found herself confused by that.

"It is my building," he said. "For now, everything is empty. It requires security clearance to get in, of course."

They walked through the empty space, to the elevators, where he entered a passcode, and the doors slid open.

They got inside.

"You live in this whole empty building."

"It will be turned into luxury apartments for others to rent. But I have been enjoying the solitude. The top floor is mine."

She thought about what he had said. How he valued his space.

"Is this just you maintaining control of an entire building?"

He looked at her. "It does not make sense to continue to do it always."

"Right."

The doors opened, and there was a small entryway, and another door that required another code.

When they were inside, her jaw dropped. The space was expansive. And there was nothing in it beyond the necessary. The kitchen was black. The floors were black and glossy, the cabinets a glossy black as well. The countertops made of graphite-colored concrete. It was opulent in a way, but also spare. The materials themselves provided the cues of luxury. The couch that stretched across the living area was black, like everything, starkly shaped. And the view of the city below was stunning. It was beginning to get dark, and the lights glowed bright from the cars, the buildings, street signs and neon advertisements.

"It's strange to me," she said, "that you prize this level of spareness quite so much, and control, and yet you live in a city that is so... Loud. And cluttered."

He laughed. "I suppose so. And yet, it allows me to keep nothing. If I want something, I go out and get it at a moment's notice. There is no need to hoard when the world is at your fingertips."

"Considering that you're a billionaire I rather thought

that you had the ability to do that even if you lived on a mountaintop."

"Perhaps. Although it would be inefficient."

"Ah. Efficiency."

"Come," he said. "I will show you to your room."

Her room.

"We won't share a room?"

She didn't know why, but the look on his face made her laugh. Well, she did know why. The stark horror there was just too funny. If a little bit insulting. "No," he said. "I prize my space."

"Right."

"We have an event tonight," he said.

"Tonight?" she asked, shocked.

"Yes. A charity event. There is a red dress in your closet. I want for you to wear that."

"You even get to choose what I wear."

"Did you want to stand there and dither over which thing to choose? Did you wish to wonder what might be appropriate?"

No. Dammit. The annoying thing was, she didn't want that. And it was helpful that he told her what she should wear.

"How long do I have to get ready?"

She would not validate him by indicating that she was grateful he had given her direction on her outfit.

"You have an hour and a half."

He opened the door to her bedroom, and clearly in-dicated she was to go inside. She did, and saw that her room was much the same as all the others, Spartan and spare. One wall was a window in its entirety. She stood there, feeling tiny and remote as she looked out over the city.

She took her phone out of her pocket, and FaceTimed Melody.

"I have a strange story to tell you," she said.

"What?" Melody asked.

She took her phone and turned it so that her friend could see the scene below.

"Where are you?"

"I'm in New York."

"New York City?" her friend asked, emphasis on each word.

"Yes," she said. "New York City. And… I'm engaged."

She flipped the phone around to face her again.

Melody's expression was wild. "Engaged? Not to that gorgeous man you brought into the coffee shop."

"The very same."

"No, well… You barely know him."

"I know parts of him pretty well," she muttered.

"You don't have to marry a man just because you slept with him," Melody said. "I don't care what the church elders say."

Noelle snorted. "That's not why I'm marrying him." Though, it was a little bit. Not because she thought she had a moral obligation to do it, but because she felt connected to him in a way that she couldn't explain. She wasn't even going to try. She couldn't even make it make sense to herself, much less her friend.

"So he's rich?"

"Yeah. Well, he's sort of the billionaire that has been trying to buy my bed-and-breakfast."

"No," Melody said.

"Yes. But we got snowed in together…"

"Real life is not a Hallmark movie," said Melody. "The evil developer stays an evil developer. I mean, the fact that he dragged you back there instead of moving to the small town is kind of making that point for me."

"Oh," Noelle said. "I know."

She went over to the closet and pulled out a red dress. It was satin and slinky, with straps that went… She didn't even know where.

"But you got engaged to him."

"I have feelings for him," she said. She sighed heavily. "I know. I know. And he hates our town. But he agreed to let me keep the bed-and-breakfast. He agreed to give my mom the payout that she wants anyway."

"What's he getting out of it? I mean, no offense. Not that you aren't a prize."

"I am definitely a prize," she said. Then she laughed. "No. I mean… He wants a baby."

Melody's forehead wrinkled. "Oh, I don't know what to do with that."

She imagined a baby. Soft and small, with Rocco's dark hair. "I've always wanted to be a mother," she said. "And… You know my mom leaving hurt. It broke something. I get to keep my bed-and-breakfast. I get to have a family. Unconventional, maybe. He's going to keep living in New York most of the year. But he says that I can go back home and stay at the bed-and-breakfast sometimes."

"So it's a marriage of convenience," Melody said.

She wished that it was that straightforward. That there were no feelings involved on her end. But there were. There were a lot of feelings.

"Yes," she said. "Of a kind. It's not that we don't have… A certain amount of passion."

Melody blinked. "Wow."

"I don't want you to think of me as some sacrificial lamb going to the slaughter when I go to his bed. I certainly went the first time with no coercion whatsoever, and no offer of marriage or saving my bed-and-breakfast on the table."

"Admittedly," Melody said. "He is the most handsome man I have ever seen."

"He really is," Noelle agreed.

She looked at the dress. "I have to go. I have to get ready for this… This thing."

"What thing?"

"A big party. Where everyone is going to be watching me and judging me next to this man, who is sophisticated and gorgeous. And deciding whether or not I'm good enough for him, I guess."

"Well, you make it sound very fun."

She suddenly realized what an interesting trap she had stepped into. Rocco had all the power. If he decided to, he could send her back home, demolish the bed-and-breakfast anyway. They weren't married yet. No agreements had been signed.

She could've come all this way only to go right back.

And it was even more impossible to imagine going back to the way things had been before now.

She had come so far, and yet, she still had nothing to hold on to, not really.

Except for him.

This wildly difficult man that had woven himself around her existence.

"I better look great in this dress."

CHAPTER TEN

HE WAS ABOUT to go in and fetch her when she emerged. And his heart nearly exited his chest, straight through his rib cage. He had never been affected so by a woman. And he couldn't quite pinpoint why it was happening now. But with or without reason she affected him all the same.

The dress was… She looked like a present. All red and satin and he wanted to unwrap her more than anything.

It was a complicated series of straps that crossed low in the front, showing her glorious cleavage.

The back was almost entirely bare, the satin hugging the curve of her rear, before cascading out around her feet like a waterfall.

She was… Everything.

"You will do," he said.

She looked at him like he was certifiable. Nobody ever did that. Nobody was brave enough. Nobody but her.

"You are beautiful," he said. "Does that fix things?"

"Why is it so difficult for you to compliment me?"

"What is difficult is finding words for what I feel." That was honest. He wasn't sure that he liked it, because he felt as if she had extracted a compromise from him. And he was determined not to be changed by this.

He wanted to build a hedge around his space, as he had done when he was a child, to keep himself protected. Pure. Controlled.

Control.

A word that cut both ways with such precision. He did not care for it.

And yet, it was what also protected him. Even while it was what had victimized him. But his control, that never failed him.

And so, his control was how he would choose to live.

"You look all right too," she said, lifting a brow.

It astonished him, the way that she was so... Resilient. Even so soundly out of water as she was. A little fish who shone brightly in spite of it all. He thought of how he had tried to chop wood and cook at the bed-and-breakfast. The way that he had tried to bend himself to care for her when she was ill. He had made a mess of everything. It had been torturous. And none of that torture was visible here, now with her.

"Let us go," he said.

He was about to put his arm out, but she closed the distance between them and held his hand. "I will probably need a coat," she said.

"Yes, of course."

He knew that one had been placed in the coat closet by the door, and he opened it up, producing a white, faux fur dress that would fall nearly to her ankles.

He put it on her, slowly. Her scent mesmerized him. The way she looked up at him. He was held in thrall for a moment. Perhaps this was what it was like when one got to know a lover. He had no experience of that. Sex was a need that he wrapped tightly in control. Because to share with someone else was to engage in give-and-take. Never his strong suit.

But perhaps this was the other side of it. The benefit. He had always imagined that one would grow bored with a lover eventually, and yet he found himself growing more and more intrigued by his.

She held his hand again as they made their way down to the front of the building, and got into the waiting limousine.

"Very fancy," she said.

They had only taken a town car from the airport.

"It is meant to give us room," he said.

Her brows lifted. "For what?"

He chuckled. "I don't know. Perhaps you could think of something."

"I have only just put this dress on. I'm not taking it back off."

He growled. He hadn't even meant to do that.

Her eyes went wide. "Feral."

"I'm not feral," he said.

"You kind of are. Strange, feral man. In the most luxurious of surroundings. And yet… You don't quite know what to do with people. Do you?"

"I am very good with people. My position demands it."

"Are you good with people, or do you find yourself in a position of power over them and they respond accordingly?"

"What is the difference?"

She shook her head and leaned back against the seat. "Nothing of note to you, I suppose."

"You mean if I did not have power, people would not treat me with deference."

She shook her head. "No. They wouldn't. And that actually has nothing to do with your personality. That's just life."

He didn't like that thought, because it made him feel powerless. It made him feel like his position in the world was tenuous. It made him feel like a small boy again. Because he could remember well what it had been like when he had no influence in his life, in his house growing up. And for just a moment, he had the flickering glance that she would not be here if he didn't have power over her life.

If he hadn't manipulated her.

He pushed that to the side, because there was no benefit to the thought whatsoever.

None whatsoever.

The car pulled up to the gala venue, a stately museum with vast steps, and pillars.

He was gratified by the look on her face. Because he was giving her something. This was an experience far outside her own, and she might not have known that she wanted it, but he would see that she benefited from it. And it didn't matter then, why she was here. It didn't matter. Because the truth was, he had the control.

He had the influence.

He got out of the car ahead of his driver opening the door, and attended to it on behalf of Noelle, taking her hand and pulling her against him as he closed the door. "You do look beautiful," he said.

Perhaps to add more to the moment. Perhaps to make her remember that it wasn't only his offer to let her keep the bed-and-breakfast that had brought her here. It was the passion between them. That was real. It had nothing to do with his influence.

It certainly had nothing to do with his soup-making skills.

"So do you," she said softly, touching the side of his face. Then he felt as if she had grabbed the thread inside of him and pulled it hard, unraveling something. He did not know what to make of that.

He did not know how to proceed. Except to walk up the steps holding tightly to her, entering the building.

There were so many women dressed in colorful dresses, and yet they remained indistinct blurs to him. The trouble was, everyone did. Even people who held influence at the event, the people that he wanted to network with, and speak to, meant so little. Because what he really wanted to do was take that dress off Noelle. To the degree that he resented that they had to go out at all. Of course, if they hadn't gone out she wouldn't have put that dress on.

Whenever someone talked to her, monopolized her attention, he resented it. It made him miss the bed-and-breakfast. It made him want to go back to the top of the secluded mountain with her where he did not have to consider anyone else ever.

It made him want to reclaim her for himself.

He hated that town. He hated that mountain. There was no reason for him to harbor fantasies about returning there. To that cluttered old house filled with dust catchers that she called knickknacks. Filled with memories that weren't his own, and never would be.

He felt himself growing impatient. And perhaps it didn't really matter if he was here at all. The business was now his to run by his own design. He no longer had to engage in endless expansion. He could simply maintain what was. Make better what existed, rather than cluttering up the earth with more resorts that nobody wanted or needed.

That was his mother's grand design, of course. It was not his, and it never would be.

So maybe it was all right that he didn't want to network. Maybe it was all right that what he really wanted to do was take Noelle straight back to his apartment.

Though there was a small amount of joy to be had when he watched her interact with the people around him. She was entirely out of her depth, and yet there was a glow about her that people seemed to find irresistible. God knew that he did.

Even as he grew jealous when other men monopolized her attention, he also felt pride that they saw what he did.

He found it increasingly difficult to keep his hands to himself. He went from holding her hand to wrapping his arm around her waist. Pressing himself against her, moving his hand over her bare back, and then kissing her neck.

"Rocco," she said.

"What?"

"We are in public."

"I find myself bored of the public," he said. "Let's go home."

Noelle had had a lovely evening, but Rocco had clearly been growing impatient. And every time he touched her it felt like he ignited a spark inside of her. Realizing the effect that she had on him, even in his environment... It emboldened her.

When they got out of the building, and into the limo, she positioned herself across the way from him. "That wasn't very polite," she said.

"What? We stayed an hour."

"Barely," she said. "And I was having a lovely time."

"I'm glad for you," he said. "But I found myself growing exceedingly impatient."

"I gathered that."

"Witch," he said.

"Hardly," she said.

But inside she felt satisfied. That he was undone. That she had this much power.

The way that his eyes glittered when he looked at her sent a shiver through her. This handsome man wanted her.

She wasn't just the only woman available at the top of a snowed-in mountain. There had been beautiful women all over that gala. He was impatient to leave with her.

She needed to hear him say that.

Because she wanted… Something intense. Something reckless tonight. She felt like when she had slipped this dress on she had put on new skin with it. Like perhaps she had uncovered new depths to herself, new layers.

Like she wasn't just Noelle, with the Christmas tree farm and the bed-and-breakfast. Unassuming and sweet.

Trying to hold together the warm, glowing images of her childhood.

Wholesome. That was what she had always been. Trying to maintain this air of wholesomeness, essentially, as she clung to a two-dimensional vision of her past.

Of her parents.

She had kept herself simple because she resented the complexity of her mother.

That was a stunning realization.

And yet, not one she needed to deal with just at the moment. What she really needed was him.

"Do you want me, Rocco?"

"Yes," he growled.

"I don't mean opportunistically. I don't mean because

I'm the woman who you decided to marry for your own convenience. I don't mean… You know, how I pointed out to you that people are nice to you because you have power over them. I don't want you to want me simply because this arrangement gave power to you. Or because we were stuck on a mountaintop."

"I could not even see the faces of the other women there. I could not track the shapes of their bodies. They were brightly colored orbs, orbiting around you. They meant nothing to me. No memory of sex means anything to me. Only the reality of you. You are correct, I am a man with exceeding power. I have trapped you with me, haven't I? Because of that, I do not have to give you my fidelity, do I? I could have left with one of those women. What would you have said? What would you do?"

"I would be hurt," she said.

"And that would only matter to me if I cared about your feelings. My point is, nothing is stopping me from taking another woman if I want her. But I do not. I want you."

That was what she needed to hear. She closed the distance between them, crossed the space, and claimed his mouth. She kissed him deep and long, as she had wanted to do all day, but had felt so disoriented, she simply hadn't. Or perhaps she had been protecting herself. But not anymore.

He was starving. She could feel it in every line of his body. The growl that exited his mouth, even though he was bound and determined to pretend that he was not feral for her.

He was.

She was.

They arrived at the penthouse too fast and too slow. And she moved away from him reluctantly, allowing him to take her hand and lead her out of the car.

She was covered by her coat. It felt cumbersome. Like too many layers, when she wanted to be naked against him.

What a strange thing to know exactly what she wanted. To be in this strange place, in a new situation, and yet to know this.

It was like an anchor, holding her fast to the earth.

What a glorious thing.

The trip up to the apartment was a blur. And when they entered, he pulled her hard against him, kissing her deep, letting her feel that iron hardness of his body, letting her feel exactly what she did to him.

He pushed the coat off her shoulders, as she began to loosen his tie.

They moved, in synchronous rhythm, to that expansive black couch.

They stood at the edge of it, her back to the window, and he began to untie the straps that held the dress to her body.

It fell away, leaving her naked except for the red high heels she was wearing. She hadn't put any underwear on beneath the dress because it simply hadn't allowed for it.

The fabric was to slippery and silky. And now she was grateful for it, because the look on his face was… That was a look that she wanted to pursue. Not just now, but maybe forever.

She felt like she was enough. She felt special.

Not just in the context of being the only woman on the mountain.

It was intoxicating.

He stripped his tie away, and shrugged his jacket off, then he began to unbutton his shirt, and she watched with rapt attention.

As he revealed that gorgeous chest, his rippling stomach. He cast the shirt to the ground, and began to undo his belt slowly, and she found her breath hitching slightly with each articulated movement. He stripped himself entirely naked, and sat on the edge of the couch, like an emperor. "Come to me," he said.

She was very aware that her back was to an open window, and that her front was to a naked man. That she wanted him, as fiercely as he wanted her.

The center of her ached. Felt hollow with the need for him.

She could feel how slick and wet she was with each step she took toward him. It didn't even occur to her not to obey. Not when obedience would lead her exactly where she wanted to go.

"Take your hair down," he said.

She reached up and quickly dashed the pins out of her hair, letting it fall around her shoulders in a wild cascade.

"Yes," he said, his voice hoarse. "Now you are feral for me."

She laughed. She couldn't help herself. Because of course she was. She always was. She had been from the beginning, hadn't she? After thinking herself tame for so many years, the truth of it was she had never met anyone who made her wild.

But he did.

And that was when she did something entirely out of character, without even thinking. She ran her hands over her aching breasts, summing the nipples, pinching herself, watching as his expression went from stormy to the black eye of a hurricane.

She let her hands move down her own waist, her hips, before pressing one down between the center of her thighs, where she touched her own slickness. Where she zeroed in on that beat of pleasure, and began to stroke herself.

"Noelle," he growled.

She didn't know who she was. Who was this woman? Bold and naked in front of a window, pleasuring herself as a man watched her. Who was this woman, in nothing but red high heels?

Who was this woman, in New York City, with a heavy diamond ring on her left hand.

She was her. That was the stunning thing. She was Noelle Holiday. All things Christmas and bright. And yet sensual and needy with him.

It was like finding herself. Like seeing herself for the very first time.

She continued to walk toward him, and she didn't have to be asked. She knew exactly what to do. She straddled his lap, bringing her slick center against his hardness. He growled, his large hands cupping her ass as he brought her forward, arching against her, rubbing himself through her slick folds.

"Mine," he said.

And she could only agree, in small, short bursts of need.

It was like heaven to have his hands on her. And she luxuriated in it. He moved them up her back, down her arms, around to cup her breasts, and his touch on her sensitized skin was so much better than her own could ever be.

He teased her, his thumbs moving over her aching peaks, and then he moved his head there, sucking her deep, biting her. She cried out, the pleasure/pain paradox making her head spin.

Making her ache for more.

He wrapped one arm tight around her waist, and gripped her chin with the other, making bold eye contact with her as he thrust himself up inside of her. She moaned, his possession thorough, complete and glorious.

And she began to move over him, as he held her steady, as he let her have the control. Was there any control to be had? She was this creature that he had made her. One of need and desire.

One of absolute earth and fire. He had broken something in her, or made something in her, she didn't know which. Perhaps it didn't matter.

There was nothing but them. All she could see were those dark eyes, gazing deep into hers. The sparkling ring on her left hand, his muscular chest, her hand against his shoulder. He whispered things against her mouth, dirty and beautiful all at the same time.

And when they went over the edge, it was together. Her nails digging into his skin as he poured himself deep inside of her.

She collapsed against him, and he lay back on the couch, still buried inside of her, his hands moving through her hair.

"Stay on the pill for a while," he said.

The comment jarred her back to reality.

"What?"

"There's no need for you to fall pregnant immediately. And… I think it would be better for you to become accustomed to this life."

Confusion twisted inside of her. "I thought that it was important…"

"This is important," he said.

The granite in his voice rebuilt something within her that had cracked only a moment ago. He didn't want to have a baby because he didn't want to be distracted from the attraction between them. She was actually happy with that. Happy to put it off for a little while.

"It would be better," he said. "Anyway. The optics. If

you waited at least a year to get pregnant, there would be no question as to why I married you."

She nodded. Except of course, if people asked questions about why they got married, and came to the conclusion it was not for love, then they would be right.

But something had certainly shifted within her.

This thing that moved her further and further away from who she was. Further and further from home.

She clung to his shoulders then, desperate. Because he was the only thing keeping her here.

On his whim, the bed-and-breakfast could go away. On his whim this relationship could end. And she would be the one left picking up the pieces. It felt hideously imbalanced. Except he wanted her.

He had said it.

This was her power.

What a strange thing, for a woman who had never wielded power in any way, but least of all this way.

"Yes. We can wait."

"Good. I think that you should spend tonight in my bed."

So she did.

CHAPTER ELEVEN

WHEN ROCCO SHOWED up to the board meeting the next day, he knew that he was going to be met with sterling opposition.

"This is how you tell us that you are engaged?" Jeremiah Ulster, one of the oldest members of the board, tossed his phone into the center of the table, pictures of him and Noelle plastered into a tell-all article. Of course, he and Noelle had told nothing. But everyone knew at this point he had been snowed in on the mountain, and they knew that she was the person he had been snowed in with. People wanted to believe in romance so desperately, that they fashioned one out of it. And that suited him just fine.

"It is not my fault that the press decided to fill in their version of the truth without my speaking to you. But, as you know, I was indisposed for a while, and could not communicate, and when Noelle and I arrived in the city last night we had an event to attend."

"You were making a show of it," Jeremiah said.

"Yes," he said. "Perhaps I was. And perhaps that will serve as a reminder that I am not a child to be scolded, whether or not my mother put you in your position or not. This is my company, and I make decisions based on what I feel is best. The expansion ends. I am to be married."

"Surely we have to approve that," Jeremiah said, and he searched around as if he was hunting for a stack of bylaws.

"You don't," Rocco said. "I simply must wed within three months of informing you. Which I shall do. And then within a year of the marriage, my wife must be pregnant, or we must be in the process of pursuing surrogacy or adoption."

"You are quite well versed," Jeremiah said.

"Because it is my life," Rocco said. "It is my life, and I will do with it what I choose. I have chosen to marry Noelle Holiday. It is my right. She is the woman that I have chosen. And I am not building a resort in Wyoming."

"What?" This came from Rosalie, another older member of the board.

"No, I am not. Because my wife, Noelle, will be preserving her family home rather than agreeing to any changes."

"You've cut a deal with her," Rosalie said. "That much is obvious."

"And what incentive would I have to do that?" Rocco asked. "She is the one who benefits from it, not me. I found that I had a change of heart up on the mountain."

"I don't believe it," Jeremiah said.

"It is not for you to believe. It is what is happening. You were all happy with my mother's mental deterioration because she gave you more power. And the eternal expansion lines your pockets. But I do not work for you. And I am not someone you can take advantage of. Perhaps it has not been clear. I am Rocco Moretti. And I will have my way."

He stormed out of the meeting, his heart hammering. He was furious. Every single one of them had a stake in the way that things had gone with his mother.

And they would pay for it. By watching their easy profits slip away. And once he had total control of everything, he would oust them. He also knew that they were going to drip feed terrible PR stories to the media. There were going to be competing narratives now. He called Noelle as soon as he got into the car.

"Oh," she said. "I didn't expect to hear from you."

"I just had a rather explosive meeting. You have to be aware that there is going to be negative press. Because the board is opposing this marriage. They have no control, but once we have a child, I can begin the process of replacing them, and they don't like that. They are going to make it sound as if this marriage is an entirely Machiavellian scheme on my part."

There was a short pause on the other end of the line. "Isn't it?"

For some reason he didn't like that. Not after the explosiveness of last night. Not after everything.

"Still. You may feel differently when you see it plastered in black-and-white. They will do their best to smear us and to smear you."

"I can handle it," she said.

"I hope that's true. Because we are going to have to ramp up our efforts. We will be attending a great many events leading up to Christmas. I'm going to get you a wedding planner, and we are going to plan a Christmas charity event."

"That's a lot," she said.

"I'm a lot. If you hadn't noticed."

"Yes," she said. She sounded sad.

Perhaps it was the reminder that all of this served a very specific purpose. He could admit, even if just to himself, that he was somewhat surprised by how jarring it was to have to contend with the fact that there was a scheme at play here. Especially when last night had felt... Like they were the only two people on earth.

"You forget," she said. "I have run a Christmas tree farm in a small town for years. I can handle intense. I can handle holly and jolly. We have nearly a month until the big day. We can accomplish a lot in that time."

"You are perfect for this," he said.

And only after he hung up the phone did he realize how true that was.

"You are perfect for this."

Noelle clung to that. Day in and day out over the next few weeks.

She started working on planning the charity event he wanted to throw. She talked about it endlessly when they would go out to different functions. And she ignored the venomous headlines that came out about them.

The tell-alls from women he had slept with before. Talking about his prowess and how cold he was.

It hurt her, to read those stories. She tried not to. Because there really was no point. It didn't benefit her in any way.

It didn't help her. It only hurt.

So she ignored them. Because he had warned her. And he had been very, very right.

Their outings together created their own fight against the narrative.

She stood by him.

She nearly had apoplexy, though, when a story came out about her mother.

The gold-digging mother-in-law who had been unfaithful to her husband before his death, and who wanted nothing more than to get a big payout. Had she in fact orchestrated this alliance between her daughter and Rocco?

The idea of her mother being that strategic was hilarious.

The revelations about the infidelity less so.

This just… It destroyed everything. Shattered her pretty childhood snow globe into thousands of pieces. Had she known anything about her own life?

She didn't know if the allegations were true or not. But Christopher Farmer, a man who lived down the road from them had given an interview in the paper about it.

That they had been lovers. He had clearly gotten a pay-out of some kind.

Noelle called her mother. "Mom," she said. "Is this true?"

"Noelle, life is complicated," her mom said. "I regret it. And your dad forgave me. It happened a long time ago."

"You just never really loved us, did you?" Noelle asked.

"I do," her mom said. "I did."

"Well, you're partying in Boca with my fiancé's money, so I guess you love how useful I am to you."

Noelle hung the phone up.

She tried to forget that happened when Rocco came home and she lost herself in his touch.

That was the one place where everything felt like it made sense.

In bed with him.

At least there she had some sanity. Or rather, a really perfect brand of insanity. There was also Melody.

And Daniela, her wedding planner, who was lovely, and quickly becoming a friend.

"Weddings are stressful for anybody," she said. "But especially so when there's this big of a circus around it."

"The board is bound and determined to mess all of this up. I'm not going to let them," she said.

Because she thought of that little boy, whose mother had controlled everything, and hadn't taken care of him at all. And that helped. When nothing else did.

Of course, nothing helped the shambles she felt like

her emotions were in, but it at least gave her the will to go on.

She found that she liked New York more than she would've imagined. Was happier there than she had thought possible. When she didn't wear makeup, and she put on a hat, nobody recognized her. Because she was only famous as Rocco Moretti's beautiful, made-up fiancée.

So when she was just Noelle, nobody looked at her. Nobody saw her. That was something that never happened at home. She couldn't be anonymous if she wanted to, and given the amount of phone calls she had gotten since the news about her mother's infidelity had been splashed all over the news, there would be no sanity to be had at home.

She understood that.

And she wanted nothing to do with that.

At Christmastime, the city was beautiful. And she found herself going to the tree at Rockefeller Center often, gazing up at it, thinking about home, and finding a way to feel nostalgic about it.

She was meeting Daniela for lunch, and to have a conversation about flowers. The Christmas event was looming, and she was feeling especially... Fraught.

It was just a lot. Everything.

She wasn't used to this. This feeling of being turned inside out, exposed. Yes, in a small town everybody knew her, which was its own issue, but there was also the issue of the way she lived her life. She didn't parade her business around. She never had. She went internal. She focused on her bed-and-breakfast. Her only sanity was him. That was her version of going internal now. Losing herself in his touch, in his arms.

She and Daniela passed by a storefront on Fifth Avenue that had exceedingly shocking lingerie outfits on the manikins in the window.

"I think I'd like to go in there," she said.

"Planning for the honeymoon?" Daniela asked.

"Or just Tuesday," she said brightly.

Because she really was this whole other person now. This woman who reveled in her sexuality.

She was cautiously amused by herself. By this change in her.

Even while there was a bit of foreboding lingering in the background. A small amount of fear that this could rebound on her. That she would be utterly entirely lost at sea if something happened to their relationship.

But it was no matter.

Because it was too late, that was the thing. She was out in the middle of the ocean, in a small inflatable raft, clinging to a rope that kept her tethered.

Rocco was the rope.

If she lost hold of him, she didn't know what would happen.

But she was already in the middle of the sea.

So she bought five different lace and transparent silk outfits, so little fabric for so much money, and she let herself enjoy it. Let herself get excited thinking about what he would do when he saw them.

What are you doing?

It was a text from Melody, right as she exited the store.

Just spent a ridiculous amount of Rocco's money on underwear.

I have to get an Italian boyfriend.

Fiancé.

And she added a smiley face for good measure.

Even with the heaviness of the media barrage, she felt buoyant.

And she followed that buoyancy down Fifth Avenue, and she and Daniela made an appointment with one another to do wedding dresses the next week.

Then she walked the rest of the way back to Rocco's penthouse, enjoying the bustle. Now that she was getting used to the rhythm of the city, she did find beauty in it.

It was different than the beauty she was born into. Different than the life she had chosen for herself.

But it was beautiful all the same.

She didn't expect to find Rocco home in the middle of the day, and yet when she got to the penthouse, he was. Standing there with his back to her, facing the scene below. His posture looked especially straight, his figure imposing with his jet-black hair ruthlessly tamed into place, and his black suit so expertly cut to the lines of his body.

But there was an aura of something radiating from him that actually frightened her.

"Rocco?"

He turned toward her, a glass of scotch in his hand. He was home in the middle of the day, and he was drinking in the middle of the day. That was a bad sign.

"What…"

"Have you not seen?"

"No. I've been out shopping with Daniela."

"Well, it is only a matter of time. They've done it."

"They've done what?"

"The board has decided, in their infinite pettiness, to publish my mother's greatest secret."

"Oh…"

And admittedly, she didn't understand why that was a problem. She couldn't say that to him, not while he looked like the very angel of death, but Rocco was amazing for what he had been through. For coming out of the life that he had been brought up in as well as he had.

He shouldn't bear any embarrassment or shame because of it.

She could see, though, that he did not feel that way.

"Rocco…"

"They published pictures of the house. The inside of the house. Of all the things. All the horrible, disgusting things, piled up past the windows. You couldn't even see outside anymore. It blocked the daylight. My mother's staff... They betrayed her. They were complicit in it. They lived in it. They enabled her, and now they have gone and exposed her. Exposed me."

"Rocco, none of it had anything to do with you. You were just a child."

"I lived in it," he said. "And you scrub your skin, and try to clean yourself, but the smell will not come out. It still doesn't. I can still... Feel it, on me like a film. Don't you understand? Nobody that lived in that house was separate from it. I am not separate from it."

"But it isn't... None of it was your fault."

"She was my mother. And... There is nothing half so horrible as hating a person for what they do to you and loving them just as fiercely. Wanting to protect them. Because even if she didn't know the full scale of how ashamed she should be, I did. I did, and I took it all on myself, onto my own shoulders. I know how wrong it was. I know how... How sick she was. But it was never out. It was not her legacy. I took that all into myself, onto myself, to avoid ever having it be something that marred her name forever, and now they have just done it."

She took her phone out, and she googled it. And there it was. Pictures. This beautiful, stately manner home, with piles of garbage as if it were a bespoke landfill.

There were rooms that had semblances of order to the stacks. Books, magazines, newspapers. But others that were simply... Indistinct mounds of trash. The kitchen... There was food everywhere. On every surface. She could imagine the smell. Why it had been so difficult for him to eat, why he couldn't just trust anything.

He was so fastidious, so clean, so perfect.

It was an assault to think of him living this way. To think of how he'd had to bear that. And even though she didn't think he should carry any of the shame, she could see that he did.

Perhaps it was very like her own shame. This feeling of not being enough to make her mother happy. Maybe he felt that too.

Because for all that he was this creature of order and authority, he had been helpless then.

The kind of man he was... It no doubt aided him.

He likely thought the world saw this and saw his failure.

"I have lived with you for nearly a month," she said. "And you do not allow me total control of your space. It is yours. You have very clear boundaries."

"Yes," he said.

"In her way, so did your mother. You could no more sweep in and control everything than I can now."

"I'm not like my mother," he said.

Horror burst in her chest. "I didn't mean it that way. I only meant—"

"Do not seek to give advice on something you can't possibly understand. You are upset because your parents had the same sort of issues that everyone has the world over. A minor infidelity, the ache of suburban ennui. Your childhood was happy. Your parents managed to hide it from you. You have any idea what I would give to have had my mother hide her psychosis from me? Rather than including me in the middle of it? Do not try to understand me. Do not seek to compare. It is an absolute injustice."

He stepped away, going into his room and closing the door firmly behind him.

And she knew there was no reaching him. Not now.

He didn't care about this…this thing that had hurt her so much and he'd used this to push her away rather than bringing them closer together.

Over the next few days it was a grim march to Christmas Eve. She didn't even try to ask him about having a Christmas tree in the penthouse. Of course he would never allow it.

It would be clutter.

And he didn't allow that, however mad he got when he felt like she was attempting to compare him to her mother.

But they had their charity event tonight, and the entire purpose of the barrage of attacks that they had been under was so that they couldn't show their faces. Was so they would decide to call off their marriage. This trial by media had one purpose. And even if Rocco couldn't do this now, she would.

He was her lifeline.

And he had denied her these past few days. He hadn't so much as spoken to her, much less touched or kissed her.

She felt alone. Adrift.

It was as awful as she had feared that it would be.

And yet she was still here, so she would still fight.

The night of the gala, she dressed up in a very fitted emerald green dress with a sweetheart neckline, one of the strapless, glorious concoctions she had bought the other day with Daniela, before everything had fallen apart, securely underneath.

If only she could feel as put together as she looked.

But not even very fancy underwear could save her from the havoc Rocco was wreaking on her heart.

CHAPTER TWELVE

HE EMERGED FROM his room, dressed meticulously, of course. But she could see the distance there. When he moved to her, he did not touch her.

She lifted her chin. "So this is how it's going to be?"

"What are you talking about?"

"You're going to let them win. This is what they wanted. They want to stop the two of us from getting married. So you're going to act in a way that's going to guarantee to drive me away, you're going to act in a way that will guarantee we appear compromised and defeated at our own charity event."

"I am not compromised or defeated," he said, a defiant light in his dark eyes.

"You won't even touch me. You don't think that people are going to notice that? You don't think that it is utterly, horribly apparent that whatever connection we have is not functioning right now?"

His lip curled. "I am in command of this."

"Then be in command of it. Don't just perform. Don't let somebody else decide how much shame you should carry." She lifted her chin. "And I don't need you to tell me what I understand and what I don't understand. I have lived with you for a month. I'm getting to know you. Maybe I didn't go through all the same things that you did. But everybody… Everybody is a little bit messed up by something. We all are. That isn't a bad thing, it isn't necessarily anybody's fault. But it is the way that it is. So no, maybe I haven't experienced the trauma that you have, but I know what it's like to have something very personal put out there for the public to see. Maybe it doesn't seem like a big deal to you, but it does to me. And you don't need to protect the pain that you feel by trying to minimize mine. You also don't need to hide. I'm here. And I'm willing to talk, to listen, whatever you need."

His black eyes remained cold, but he looked her up and down. "I don't need anything."

"Of course not. You don't need people. You are Rocco Moretti. An island." She felt terrible, for saying that. After everything he had been through. She pinched the bridge of her nose. "You are not a small boy stuck in your bedroom anymore." She looked up at him. "I'm sorry. I'm sorry that they dragged all of that out. I'm sorry that they've dredged all of this up. It isn't fair."

He looked… Regretful then. "No," he said. "I'm the one that is sorry. I was completely unsympathetic when these things were dragged out about your family. I was entirely cold about it. I did compare it both to my own pain, and to my own goals. And your pain meant nothing in light of them. I didn't care if past lovers talked about our sexual encounters, because I don't feel… I chose that. At least. You have to stand by your choices. But now that something I have no control over has been brought out for public consumption, I get it. I feel it. And I also feel regret, for not understanding before. For giving you no sympathy. I at least chose this. I knew on some level that there could be consequences for it. But I dragged you into this, and this is not your life. I was born into a life where aspects of me will be a public consumption. You weren't."

"No," she said. "I have no experience with it. But as long as you… As long as I didn't feel completely cut off from you, it was bearable. The past few days haven't been."

He looked as if he didn't know how to respond to that. And so he didn't. That was the best that she could read of him.

If he didn't know, he simply wouldn't. And it was okay, because what she could see, what she understood was that her words had changed something inside of him. She would cling to that. So he moved near her, and he looped his arm through hers. And that was affirmation of something.

"Come along, *cara*. We will make it a night to remember."

Looking at the pain that he had caused Noelle created no small amount of shame inside of him. But he had work to do. He had to make sure that this charity event went off without a hitch. He had to prove that he was untouchable. He had to reclaim his control.

To prove that they would not have a win over him. It wasn't that he doubted that. It was only that he was not used to having another person present when he was contending with anything. Having her in his house, in his life, was unprecedented.

And it made him have to consider things in a way he had not before. He had hurt her feelings.

He held on to her the whole way down to the car, and then into the car. He was aware that they were having their photograph taken, but that was not why he held her.

When they arrived at the venue, an outdoor garden, heated by a large rig set up all around, with lights strung above them, he was amazed.

"You planned this?"

"Yes," she said.

"How did you even know where to begin?"

"I might be a small-town girl, but there's nothing I know or love more than Christmas. Or a big Christmas event."

There was a large Christmas tree at the center, reaching up past the string lights, the angel on top glittering brightly.

For some reason, it hit him square in the chest. They'd had so many things in their house, but never a Christmas tree. Never anything that was there with purpose or beauty. It was all ugly, desperate consumption.

This was not clean or spare. It was resplendent. Glittering.

It did not disgust him.

It made him feel something.

And he had no idea where to put it or what to do with it.

There were so many people waiting to speak to her, to congratulate her.

When he had chosen her to be his wife he had not imagined that she would shine on this level. She had been dragged through the mud. The media had been merciless to her.

And yet, here she was, with the glow on her face that could not be contained.

How could he have shut down as he did? When she deserved his unending praise?

This was his pattern, he supposed. When he felt out of control. When life felt out of his control.

He could not lock himself in a bedroom anymore, because he was not alone.

You would be the one freezing her out. And in that way, you would be like your mother.

He tried to push that thought to the side. He had been angry when she had drawn parallels between himself and his mother. But he couldn't deny that they existed. It was becoming harder and harder to do so.

Control.

What a strange thing that control could take such different shapes, and essentially be from the same root.

The need to hoard, the need to consume, the need for space, the need for nothing.

It was only through her eyes that he could see the similarities. And clearly.

He pushed that thought to the side, because he didn't need to have it tonight. Tonight was about her triumph. Tonight was about showing the world what they really were.

No. It's not about showing the world what you really are. Your relationship is alive. It is for convenience...it is for business. You know that.

Except it didn't feel like it was only that. He had missed her these past days. He had denied himself her body.

Because he had been so disgusted with himself. Because those pictures, that story, had brought up the depths of his shame. Had left him feeling unclean. And then his own reaction to her had made him feel even worse.

Even more unworthy of her. And then she had appeared, in that dress, her determination a ring of light around her.

How could he be any less than she was?

How could he give less than she gave?

Nobody at the party brought up any of the news articles. Of course they wouldn't, not here. No one who had been given an invite to this was lying in wait. But that would not always be the case.

There would be times when they had to confront animosity, when they would have to confront the sneering delight of people who enjoyed their embarrassment. But thankfully it was not tonight.

She deserved this night. She deserved everything.

He did not dance. It wasn't in his nature. And yet when

other couples went out to the dance floor he found himself compelled to do the same. With her.

He went to her, and reached out his hand. "Dance with me."

He let himself get drunk on her. The touch, the exhilaration of spinning with her on the dance floor. He let everyone around them fade away. He let himself feel the magic, the kind of joy he had never let himself feel around Christmas.

At the end of the evening, at the end of their last dance, she stretched up on her toes and kissed his lips, in front of everyone. "Merry Christmas."

CHAPTER THIRTEEN

SHE FELT THE intensity of what they had just experienced wrapping all the way around her skin. She didn't know what changes had been happening inside of him, but she could feel them. Like electricity crackling over his body. And when they got into the car to go back home, her breath exited her body as she caught his eyes across the seat. "A job well done," he said.

"Thank you."

"You were a triumph. In spite of everything. I was an ogre."

"Only a little bit."

"I'm sorry. I'm sorry that when you met me we were snowed in on a mountaintop, and it might have seemed like I was… Something that I'm not."

"How do you think you seemed?"

He laughed. Hard. "Normal?"

"You didn't know how to heat up a can of soup. You did not seem normal, Rocco." She closed the distance between them and put her hand on his thigh. "I came with you anyway."

He looked at her, his expression charged.

And yet again, she had the feeling that he didn't know quite what to say, so he wasn't going to say anything at all.

Instead, he claimed her mouth with his. Ruthless, hard. And it was a claiming. He pushed his fingers into her hair, knocking the pins out, and letting it fall loose.

She was breathless. Undone by it and him.

He kissed her until she couldn't breathe. Bit her bottom lip. Left her mouth swollen and aching with need.

When they arrived at the penthouse, it was all they could do to get out of the car. All they could do to make it up to the penthouse.

She had seduced him. Had teased him and tormented him before. But this was different. He was claiming her. Utterly and completely. His touch was rough, and exciting.

He tore her dress away from her body, and revealed the surprise she had on underneath. "What is this?" he growled.

"I got this for you. Days ago. But since you weren't touching me, you didn't know."

"I know now," he said, lowering his head and sucking at the tender flesh of her breast, hard. Then he bit her, leaving a mark behind. She loved it. She encouraged him. Because he was claiming her body for himself, and that was what she wanted. She didn't want to be adrift. She wanted him to hold on. She wanted everything.

He tore at the lace. She didn't tell him how expensive

it all was. It thrilled her that he was destroying it. That it inflamed him enough that he couldn't be patient.

She responded in kind. She ripped at his white shirt, at his tie, she undressed him all backward, her hands growing desperate. Then she leaned in and bit the muscle on his chest. He gripped her chin, forcing her face up, claiming her in a hard kiss.

She loved it. It was everything. So was he.

This was no gentle coming together. No soft Merry Christmas. No snow falling outside on evergreens. It was a storm. The kind that left you isolated on a mountain. The only two people in the world. The kind that toppled trees and power lines, the kind that caused landslides.

That was what they were.

Even here in this land of glass and steel, they were elemental. He clung to her hips, kissing his way down her body, pushing her back against the wall as he parted her thighs and began to lick her deep. He gave no quarter. He took her to the heights again and again, made her cry out her need.

"Again," he growled, pushing two fingers within her and thrusting.

She came again, holding on to his shoulders, leaving blood behind where her fingernails dug in deep.

He pulled her down, wrapping her legs around his torso as he stood them both up, pressing her down onto the sofa and entering her in one swift stroke. It was brutal. It was magic.

It was the damn season of cheer and happiness and joy, and she cried out a hosanna at the top of her lungs.

When it was over, she was spent and breathless. She kissed him on the chest, and looked at his profile, hard cut and glorious in the darkness of the penthouse.

"I used to be a nice girl," she whispered.

"And now you're not?"

She leaned in and kissed his chest. "No. I am obsessed with sex. And you."

"You could pick a better obsession."

"Do you think so?"

"Yes," he said. "I do."

"Too bad. Obsession works in mysterious ways."

"Good for me, I suppose."

He rolled so that he was over the top of her, looking down at her, his dark eyes burning with intensity. And that was when she realized, it wasn't simply another half of herself that had come to the fore. It wasn't simply that she had found a part of herself that she had never known before.

Being with him had changed her. Fundamentally.

It made her more assertive. It made her more sexual. It made her want things that she had never wanted before. It made what had been so important only a couple of months ago feel like a distant memory.

Being with him had changed her. It changed what she thought about. It changed what she ate, and where she was willing to live.

It upended every plan that she had ever had about herself. It was incredible.

She reached up and touched his face. And right then she knew. With a certainty. With a spark.

It was love.

She had fallen in love with him.

By inches. In hours and minutes and days. In his eccentricities, in his revelations. In the things that she learned about herself when she was with him.

The way that he made her feel. The way that he made her want to. The way that he was.

She loved him, and it was a stunning, stirring realization.

And it was a terrifying one. Something she didn't know what to do with right then. Something so deep that she knew she couldn't simply say it.

Because the problem with love was that it could be very real, and still not be enough.

At one time her mother had loved her father, that much she was certain of.

But she had folded herself into a life that she apparently hadn't wanted.

And slowly, very slowly, everything had degraded over time.

She had betrayed the man that she once loved, because she was still searching for something else. It scared her. That realization.

That you could think you wanted something, and be so very, very wrong.

And it reminded her again of that feeling of being adrift. That feeling of being evolved. Like a creature who used to be at home entirely in the water, and had learned to walk on land, but still craved the sea. An amphibian. Not really one or the other. She wondered if that was love. Finding yourself trapped in the middle of two worlds, never being able to fully inhabit either anymore. That was the scary thing. That the change was the sort that left her destined to be unsatisfied.

He wanted to live with her half the time. He wanted to allow her a chance to go back home. To raise their child in a small town.

Being away from him she would never feel whole.

Being entirely away from Holiday House, she would never be whole.

That was the bargain that she had made.

It was the impossibility of loving him. Or maybe of loving altogether. A series of compromises that left you only ever half alive.

"You are thinking," he said.

"I'm sorry. I'll stop."

"You don't need to stop."

"I probably should."

She kissed his neck, and scooted to the side just a bit. He lay down next to her. "Maybe we should get a Christmas tree," he said.

"It is eleven thirty on Christmas Eve."

"I'm a billionaire."

No sooner had he said that than he was on his phone.

And a record thirty minutes later, a Christmas tree was being placed in the center of the penthouse.

Pre-lit and glowing.

The delivery crew had left behind a box of ornaments.

"We should decorate it," he said.

Oh, yes. She loved him. Looking at him as he said that, with absolute earnestness, she was certain.

You can find a way. Just maybe. But still, she didn't speak of love out loud. Instead, she looked at him, at the Christmas lights reflected in his eyes as he hung the ornaments up on the tree, and she hoped.

As a child, she had a life that had seemed perfect.

But it hadn't been real.

It hadn't been real.

But this was. That much she knew. If she never knew anything else, then she knew that.

And she would just have to hope that the sort of magic that had enticed him to get a Christmas tree would bloom into the sort of magic that would keep them happy forever.

CHAPTER FOURTEEN

Slowly, signs that another person lived in his home began to creep in. It wasn't only the Christmas tree. That was gone by the day after Christmas. He had to have some respects for his own rules. But she began to cook for him, which meant keeping food in the house, rather than simply ordering up every time he wanted something.

She collected pots and pans and other gadgets.

There were places for everything. It was clean.

And yet, sometimes something would be left in a place that he didn't leave it, and it was a bit jarring.

He wasn't accustomed to it.

He didn't hate it.

She was… Changing things inside of him fundamentally. Making him want to change, to compromise, even. To find a way to be close to her, and not simply shut away in a fortress.

And he didn't know what to do with that.

She had a binder with all of her wedding plans in it, and he came home one day to find it all spread out on a new coffee table in the living room.

She was sitting there, chewing on a pen and looking at things. "I don't think there are enough flowers."

He lifted his brow. "Have you met me?"

"My wedding isn't going to be minimalist." She sighed. "I do wish we could have it at the Christmas tree farm."

She sounded wistful. And the truth was, he was in this moment the same man who had demanded that a Christmas tree be delivered at eleven thirty at night on Christmas Eve, and they could easily have their wedding at the Christmas tree farm. But for some reason, he didn't want to allow it. For some reason, it felt like too much of a shift. Too much of a compromise.

"If only," he said. "But the venue is booked."

She looked up at him and squinted. "Of course. I mean, I would think that with money like yours the real barrier is that you want to impress the people who are coming with a city venue?"

"You are quite comfortable spending my money," he said.

She drew back as if wounded. He hadn't meant to hurt her. He did that sometimes.

He was... He only knew how to be alone, he supposed. But she was here now, and he had to learn to be with her. He wanted to learn.

"Sorry," she said. "I didn't mean to imply that the cost didn't matter."

"No," he said. "I'm the one who was mistaken. I shouldn't have said it like that. I did not mean it."

"Oh."

She looked around. "I made a little bit of a mess."

"You live here," he said, though he said the words with some difficulty.

"You almost mean that!" she said, laughing just slightly and he felt some of the tension in him ease.

The problem was, he often felt caught between his desire to maintain his boundaries, and his desire to give her whatever she wanted. Whatever would keep her with him.

He suddenly felt an overwhelming sense of urgency. To keep her with him. To do the right thing. If he didn't, he would be left alone again, and now he had changed so much he did not think he could face it.

What an uncomfortable thing.

To have changed so much he could no longer find solace in solitude.

To not have yet changed enough to be all that she needed.

He felt very resentful, then, of the childhood he had spent in isolation. Because he blamed that, more than anything, for his inability to figure out what to do with her now.

And it hadn't mattered. Until he had wanted to keep somebody with him, it hadn't mattered. She was right, he had gone around wielding power, money and influence, and that had compensated for his lack of people skills. For his inability to compromise. For the mountain of trauma that existed inside of him that he had to scale every single day.

He didn't know how to cross that threshold with her. He didn't know how to fix it.

There were moments when everything was perfect. Then there were moments like this, where it felt like there was something missing between them. Where it felt like there was a gap that he could not close.

"It is not a money issue," he said. "But I wish to be married in the city. However, everything else regarding the wedding planning is up to you. If you wish to go maximalist, then I will give you my blessing."

She looked up at him, her eyes glittering with a kind of joy that he wasn't certain he had ever seen on another person's face. There was something so genuine about her. She seemed to feel everything. It was intoxicating. Astonishing.

He wanted to capture that. Keep it with him always. Because sometimes he disappointed her, and he was so keenly aware of that. And then moments later, this.

"We should go away," he said.

"Where?"

"Italy," he said. "I have seen where you grew up."

"You really want to go back…"

He lifted a shoulder. "I love Italy." Though the truth was a little bit more complicated. He tried to find a way to untangle it inside of him, to untangle it in his mouth so that he could explain it. "Parts of it are entirely divorced from the harder parts of my childhood. I would not go back to that house. But… Lake Como is beautiful. Milan."

"I don't have a passport," she said.

"You don't need one. Or rather, I will arrange everything. And you needn't concern yourself. You are traveling with me, and you will be taken care of."

That was a promise. One that extended well beyond just this trip. He would take care of her. She had entered into this agreement without full understanding of who he was or what it could cost to be with him. He owed her that much. She was going to be the mother of his child, after all. And more than that… There was something indescribably pure about her. Something that he had never experienced growing up. An optimism, a capacity for hope, that he simply did not possess.

He did not want to be the reason the light left her eyes. He did not want to be the thing that extinguished her hope.

He wanted to protect her. He could imagine himself easily as a knight in shining armor, wielding a sword and stepping between her and any imagined enemies.

Though the odd and instant picture that came to mind was himself, pressing the tip of the sword against his own throat. As if he was potentially the biggest threat.

She was everything he was not, and he had identified that from the first moment of illicit attraction.

Did that mean he would be the one to crush her?

No. Not if he decided he would not.

"When?"

"Now," he said.

"I have... Some appointments with Daniela."

"They can be rearranged. If you don't mind, of course." Compromise. He had done it. He was quite proud of himself.

"All right. If you're sure it's okay."

"It's more than okay. It is good. You deserve..." Everything. She deserved everything.

"What?" she asked, her eyes filled with humor.

"You deserve a break," he said. "Because being here, being in the media, I know it has been difficult for you." He hesitated. "You didn't know that your mother had an affair, did you?"

She shook her head. "No. I was convinced that she loved my father. I thought he was the one keeping her at home, and that I was the reason she left. But more and more, I realize that everything around me just wasn't true."

"I am sorry that I said what you went through wasn't difficult. I know that it was. I know that it is. I cannot imagine what it's like to have a happy childhood. But to have a happy childhood and have it proved to be an allusion..."

"It wasn't," she said softly. "In some ways. The truth is, they worked to make it a happy childhood for me. It's just that they weren't happy, I don't think. I'll never know my dad's side of things. That makes me sad. The realization that I will never really know him. My mother claimed that he knew about the affair. But how? How could he let that go? And why? Was it only for me? Did he love her that much. Did he love the facade of our family that much? I can never ask him. I feel like I'm just now realizing my parents were whole people, and it is too late for me to treat my dad like that. It is too late for me to really understand. It's a terrible thing to regret."

He felt that lodge somewhere at the center of his chest. The concept that his mother had been a whole person. Tormented, obviously, by tricks in her mind. By mental illness that had held her in such a tight grip that she had not been able to live better, not for herself or for him.

He cleared his throat. "I can imagine."

"But yes, I would like a break. This has been the most eventful couple months of my life. And I run a Christmas tree farm. So when I tell you that December can be pretty eventful…"

"I am quite certain," he said.

"You don't esteem my Wyoming wisdom."

He shook his head. "On the contrary. I do very much. Your perspective is so different than mine, and yet somehow, it brings me back around to interesting conclusions."

"Well. I'm glad to be interesting."

"Always."

He had a home in the mountains outside of Milan, and they flew there directly, with Noelle exclaiming about the private jet the whole time. And he wanted to hang on to that infectious excitement.

He wanted to hang on to her.

To give her whatever was required. He watched her face avidly when they landed and drove through the city. As she looked at all the sites. He wanted her to be pleased. To be invested in this place that he had come from.

And even more so, he wanted her to find his house beautiful. Because it was hers now too.

He reminded her of that when they went through the wrought iron gates and up to the elaborate stone facade. He never went here.

He had bought it as part of his expansion efforts. A property to add to his portfolio, and nothing more.

It was furnished in far too classical a fashion for his tastes. It bordered on cluttered, in his opinion. But because of the nature of the historic origins of the home, he had not changed anything in it. The designer of the place would have keeled over in horror had he done so. And it was more an investment, than a place for him to actually visit. An effort at keeping a hand in his homeland, rather than something that existed for him. But she would like it. It was the closest thing to Holiday House that he possessed. Because it was a time capsule of his family. Of their legacy.

A replica of what the house he grew up in could have been had his mother not let it decay under the weight of her illness.

He knew another nudge of discomfort.

Like he was on the verge of truths clicking into place, but he didn't quite want them to.

He ground his teeth together.

And then he turned his focus to Noelle.

"This is extraordinary," she breathed.

"I hear they decorated quite magnificently at Christmas."

"You haven't seen it decorated?"

He shook his head. "No. I don't often come here."

"I would love to see it at Christmas. But why decorate it if you're not even here?"

"There is a full staff. And I believe people rent it out for parties and the like."

"Oh," she said. "I suppose as a property developer you own all kinds of places that you never really go to."

"Yes. Though… Come inside."

They approached the ornate double doors, a dark walnut with brass handles, and they opened for them. Two staff members one on either side, holding them in place. "This is meant to replicate my family home."

A glint of pleasure lit her eyes. "Oh. Thank you for showing me this."

He looked at it through her eyes. He did not see dust and clutter. Rather the velvet furniture with its ornate wooden scrollwork suddenly became beautiful to him. The large, heavily framed paintings on the wall took on new life. Became a window into another time. Into the vision of the artist. Not simply a relic that would be better off in a bin than taking up space.

What was it that she did to him? It was untold.

It was completely unfathomable.

"It's incredible," she said. "I love it."

"I'm glad that you do. We will stay here for a time. There is… A beautiful train ride through the Alps, I can take you there."

He hadn't realized until this moment that his desire to keep his life so spare, so filled with space, kept him isolated. Had kept him closed off from beauty, from joy. Being with her…he felt so close to something new that he could just about feel it. Not quite.

He wanted to feel it.

He wanted to have something now, so that he could give it to her. It suddenly felt essential.

That if perhaps he could find a way to make her happy enough, it might spill over into himself.

They rested well that night in a bed he would've normally been scathing of. For all its extra pillows, and drapery around it. He had nothing scathing to say about it, especially not given what had happened between the two of them in that bed.

She was a vixen and a sex goddess, and at the same time, irrevocably his. It filled him with wonder.

He had arranged for them to have their own glass railcar attached to one of the luxury liners that traveled between Italy and Switzerland through the mountains. It also had their own luxury sleeping accommodation. The train was not a high-speed train, rather it was designed to move slowly and allow the rider to take in the majestic view of the Alps all around them.

Their car had glass walls and a glass ceiling, and was

outfitted with blankets, a table, and several places for them to sit and enjoy the view.

When they boarded, they were served hot chocolate with marshmallows, and Noelle immediately curled up in a large reclining seat, a blanket over her knees. She clutched the hot chocolate mug and looked up at him. And he felt not alone in a way that was profound.

He sat beside her. He had no interest in hot chocolate or blankets. Both were sweet and soft in ways that he could never be. But she wanted them. So he embraced them.

She looked at the mountains as they crept slowly down the track, and he looked at her. At the way the sun shone on her hair. The way her skin was illuminated by the fresh white snow.

"This is incredible," she said, snuggling against him.

"Yes," he agreed. "It is."

"I love mountains," she said. "This reminds me of Wyoming. Of the Grand Tetons. And yet I don't and I can never tire of mountains. It doesn't make them commonplace. It's stunning."

"I cannot remember what it feels like to love things. I… Have never been fascinated by nature because I cannot control it. And as far as what I bring into my home…"

"I know."

"You make me wish that I did," he said, an ache suddenly expanding in his chest. "You make me wish… I wish I could feel the things that you do. But I can watch you feel them, and that is nearly as good."

She looked at him, a smile curving her lips. "Why don't you feel them?"

"It's not that simple. It's not I…" He had the realization that in order to fix some of the issues with where he was now he would probably have to go back to when they started. And the idea of that was… Unbearable.

So he would watch her. He would feel it through her. Because that felt manageable, at least. Because it felt good.

They took their luxury dinner in the car with the lights dimmed, so that they could see the stars up above them.

And when they retired to bed, they found it plush and lovely, walls closed in to offer privacy, but the ceiling glass so that they had the view.

He stripped her slowly, kissing her neck, the lovely curve of her shoulder, her breast.

If he was to have one possession in all of his life, he decided it needed to be her.

He could say whatever he needed to to keep her with him. He could give her pleasure in all the ways he desired most.

She would not live in her little town for half the year, though. That would not work. Not before they had a child, and not after.

She had to stay with him.

But he would make her happy. He could show her all these things. He could spend a lifetime capturing her wonder like fireflies in a jar, enough for her, and enough for him.

He could.

He kissed his way down her body, down to her hip bone. To that glorious tangle of curls between her legs. He loved the taste of her.

He loved the way she cried out when he licked her. It was carnal, and yet it felt holy in a way that he would never be able to explain. He didn't have to. Because he was Rocco Moretti, above all else. And she might have bewitched him in more ways than one, but it didn't change the foundation.

He could have it all ways.

He could be this with her, and the ruthless business-man he had become.

The one that kept that lonely little boy locked in a bedroom light-years behind him.

And he would think of none of it now, because her sighs filled the room, and her flavor coated his tongue. And that was enough.

More than enough. Any more would simply be hoard-ing.

One did not need everything. That, he supposed, was the root of that illness. The need to have it all.

He would have bits and pieces. Here and there. It would be enough.

He laid her down on the bed, and thrust inside of her, watched as her expression contorted to one of wonder. Felt it echo inside of him.

With nothing but moonlight pouring down over them,

he claimed her. Over and over again. He made a promise. To make her happy.

He kissed her, with everything inside of him, and he thought that maybe it would do something to ease the ache in his chest. It didn't. It only got worse. But she was with him. She was with him still.

He thrust hard, fast, taking them both to the peak. And he swallowed her cry of need, so that it met his growl of completion.

He gathered her against his body, after they had found their release, and held her there. Their hearts beat in tandem, and he closed his eyes.

He was on the edge of something.

Something.

As he drifted off to sleep, the last image that filtered through his mind was of him, locking her in a room with him. So that she could never leave.

So that he would always have her.

Always.

CHAPTER FIFTEEN

NOELLE HAD NEVER been so happy.

Italy was beautiful. They had stayed in his house in Milan for a while after the train trip, and then they had gone on to Lake Como, then to Florence. Then on to Rome. It wasn't anything like the quiet life she had imagined for herself, but it was magical.

It was because of him.

She realized that her concept of home had shifted.

Rocco Moretti now felt like home. More than Wyoming ever had.

Even more than Holiday House. It was terrifying how quickly something like that could shift. Terrifying just how glorious a shift like that could be. If she had been told a few months ago that her whole life would change, she would have been sad about it. But now she realized that change wasn't always bad. Sometimes it was simply the right time.

Sometimes, you were ready for it.

That was astonishing.

After a month overseas, though, she was beginning to feel like she wanted to visit home. It had been three months.

Three months in total since she had seen Melody, since she had been back in her familiar territory.

Just a small visit would be nice.

It was the strangest thing, because she had a deep level of intimacy with him, and yet there were some things she still felt afraid to approach him about at times. The way he handled his issues around his childhood being the biggest, because last time it had been such a disaster. He talked about things, but she always felt reluctant to push when he wasn't the one leading.

It was because there was something under the surface, and she couldn't quite put her finger on it, but it was beginning to fill her with a sense of disquiet that she didn't quite know how to manage.

She could tell him that she loved him, of course. Take the pane of glass she felt like was between them sometimes and shatter it. Test to see if it was her fault. If her not being able to tell him the truth of her feelings was why sometimes she felt distant from him.

It was a beautiful day, and the apartment they occupied in Rome had the most stunning view. In the evenings, they sat out on the balcony, and looked at the city below.

She had a new appreciation for cities. She didn't think they would ever feel like home, but now that she had been to a few, she could appreciate that they were all different. That they had different rhythms, different personalities.

She really did love Rome.

The history, the iconic sites, the food.

She loved listening to Rocco speak Italian. She tried

to learn a little bit herself. It had turned into an extremely dirty lesson. He had taught her words that she didn't think she could ever repeat in polite company. But that she used on him with impunity, whispering in his ear when they were at restaurants, or galleries. So why couldn't she say the one thing she probably needed to say most?

Because of the illusion.

That realization stunned her. Astonished her. She stood there, on their balcony, looking out at the city, realizing that she was afraid.

That it was terribly, terribly worrying that someday, she would say the wrong thing to him. That she would uncover the fact that this happiness wasn't real. Just like her childhood. Because you could be blissful, and not realize the people around you weren't.

That filled her with panic. It made her feel like her little boat was adrift, not connected to the shore.

No. She was fine. And Rocco wasn't her only anchor. She had Snowflake Falls. She had Wyoming and Holiday House, and friends. She just had to remember that. She had been lost in a haze, and it had been lovely. But she had perhaps let herself become too comfortable with this part of her life.

Maybe she needed to remember to anchor herself.

So she went and found him, lounging on the couch in the living room, and she decided to crawl on top of him, folding her hands and resting them palms down on his chest as she looked up at him. "Hi," she said.

She could feel his body hardening. And she smiled.

"Hello," he said, wrapping his arm around her waist.

"I wanted to talk to you," she said.

"This does not feel like a prelude to talking," he said.

"How very rude," she said. "As if me pressing my body against you could only be an invitation for one thing, and not conversation?"

"You know how it is between us," he said. He held her chin, and she looked at him. She wanted to freeze time. She wanted to make it so that this moment was the only moment. Nothing after it, nothing before. Nothing to worry about.

"What?" he asked.

"Nothing I… Except something. I need to go home for a while."

He frowned. "Why?"

"I just… I miss everybody. I miss home. I'd like to actually invite people to the wedding in person. Just maybe spend a little time getting back to myself…"

"You don't need to leave," he said.

"Rocco, I have other parts to my life. I still own a bed-and-breakfast. I need to go and check on things."

And she needed to reclaim old parts of herself, but she wasn't going to say that. Especially not when the expression he was treating her to was so stormy.

"You can come with me," she said.

Though she did think that might be defeating the purpose.

"You don't need to leave," he said. "And in fact, now

that we are on the subject, I no longer think it is a feasible idea for you to live away from me for half the year."

She agreed, actually, but she wanted to know why he thought that.

"Why is that?"

She was so close to him, she could feel his heart beating beneath her hands, she could see his chest rise and fall with each breath. And she could see the tangle of emotion in his eyes. The confusion there. He didn't know the answer. And she already knew that when Rocco didn't know, he simply didn't speak.

He didn't share, he shut down. Shut parts of himself away.

"Rocco," she said. "Please… Just tell me. Tell me what the problem is?"

"There is no problem," he said. "It is only that I need you in my bed, so I cannot have you away."

She stepped closer to that glass pane that existed between them, and she pressed against it, taking the chance that it might crack.

"Is that all I am? Am I simply sex to you?"

"Of course not," he said.

"Then what else am I?"

"It isn't that simple. I cannot simply… Name all of these things. But you know that you are an important part of my life."

"You're an important part of mine. I don't want to be away from you half the year either, but we are going to have to work some things out. Because me keeping the bed-and-breakfast was part of our marriage arrangement."

It was the wrong thing to say. He growled, and rolled her off him, safely onto the cushion of the couch, as he stood, pushing his fingers through his hair. "I see. And you remind me of our agreement now, is that it? Because that is why you're here, isn't it? You are here because you want me to let you keep your bed-and-breakfast."

"I'm here because you have to get married to appease the terms of your mother's will. Has that changed?"

He looked at her again, with that same conflicted look. Why wouldn't he just say it. Why wouldn't he tell her what he was feeling. It didn't make any sense.

"I… I have no words for you, Noelle. You are being impossible."

"I'm not being impossible. And here's an idea, you can say some words, and if they are the wrong ones, you can try to find some right ones. It's all right."

"What's the point?"

"I need to… I need to understand you. Because I can't… I can't live life thinking that everything is okay between us and then randomly finding out that it isn't."

"I see. So when I am not my mother, I am your mother."

"That's not fair," she said.

"I think it is."

Maybe this was what she had sensed, this fight. This unrest between them. Maybe this was the disquiet that she felt.

She hated it. And yet, she didn't quite know what to do about it.

She wondered if it had to happen. If they had to have this discussion.

What about you? Are you ever going to tell him? You're demanding information from him, and yet you're keeping plenty to yourself.

But he was so important. She couldn't mess it up.

He was integral. If she took a risk, then she might lose everything. She had accepted this change, and she couldn't endure another one. She couldn't lose him.

Because she had chosen him. And chosen this life with him.

And what if all it ever is to him is an arrangement. What if it's only sex? And you fall deeper and deeper into love with him, and you have a child, and then that child leaves, and then he leaves you. What if he has affairs?

She had to know.

She had to know.

Her heart was thundering so hard it made her sick.

"I do not wish for you to be away from me," he said. "I want to keep you." His words were feral and fierce, and they tugged at her soul.

It felt so big. So impossibly big.

And she had just wanted to be a simple girl who lived on top of the mountain. She hadn't asked to fall in love with a man that was bigger than any mountain she had ever seen.

She hadn't asked to live an extraordinary life. She had wanted safe. She had wanted ordinary.

No, you didn't. You never did. Or you would've never left. You would never have touched him. He was an invitation to risk the entire time. Because you're not going to live like your mother.

No. She wasn't. She had been worried that love would be an endless series of compromises, but she had a feeling it was only if you didn't speak the truth to the one that you loved.

That meant she had to.

She had to.

"I love you, Rocco."

He looked at her, something like granite in his dark gaze.

"You…?"

"I love you. I realized it a while ago. But I didn't know how to tell you. I didn't want to disrupt what we have. But I… I love you."

"I don't know how to give you that," he said.

"I don't think that's true. I think you do. I think you can, I think…"

"You don't know," he said. "You don't know… I don't love you, Noelle. I fantasize about putting you in a room and locking you in there. Keeping you. Because I am like my mother, I suppose. In all the ways that matter.

"I need to control everything and everyone around me. I need… That's why I can't let you out of my sight.

I can't bear it. I brought you to Italy to make you happy. Because I want you to stay with me."

"I'm happy with you," she said slowly. "I promise you that I am. I am happy with you, Rocco, but I also need to have other things in my life. You cannot be everything to me. That is far too dangerous of a proposition for me."

"You are the only thing that I have," he said.

"One billion dollars, and you. A thousand properties, and you. And if I had to choose to keep one, it would be you. But that isn't love. It's like a sickness inside of me. And it grows, more and more by the day. I don't want you to leave. I don't want you to have a bed-and-breakfast. I want to keep you so happy that you forget that you ever had a life with anyone else."

"Rocco…"

His eyes were wild, and she knew that what he was saying was true, but there was a fury in it. One that she couldn't even see the bottom of. He was angry. With himself, possibly. With her.

With everything.

"We can talk about this…"

"No. It's unbearable. You… You need to go home." He forked his fingers through his hair. "I need you gone."

"What?"

"I need you to go. Because this growing thing inside of me is… It's the thing that I'm most afraid of. And I will trap you with me. In my room. There will be no boundaries, there will be no escape. I won't do it to you."

"You can't make my choices for me."

"The hell I can't. Because I'm making them for me too. I need things to go back to the way they were. There is… There is something… I can't put my finger on it, I can't name it, but ever since you came into my life something inside of me has shifted, and I can't figure out how to put it back."

"It's the same for me. It's love. It changed me. It made me want different things."

"If you wanted different things you would never have asked to leave."

"No, I would have. Because it is still part of me. But so are you. Love doesn't have to destroy everything that you are. It just makes you more."

"Not me. It is destroying me."

Love. He said it was destroying him. Which meant that he must feel it. But he wouldn't admit it. He was absolutely terrified, and she could see it. This brave, mountain of a man.

Was afraid of her. Afraid of what she made him feel.

"You said you wanted to feel the happiness that I felt. The wonder that I felt, can't you try to feel the love that I feel."

"No," he said. "Please… Do not ask me to."

"Rocco… Don't ask me to go."

"The damage is done," he said. "I have ruined us both. The papers have already run all the stories and…"

"So don't send me away."

"It is one or the other," he said. "Either I want to hoard, or I want nothing. And I need to go back to wanting nothing. I need to go back to when it all felt simple. When I figured out how to need no one."

"This isn't about you wanting to lock me away. This is about you being afraid of needing me. Because your mother left you alone, and you couldn't count on her and…"

"You are not my psychiatrist. Do not seek to tell me what is in my heart or in my mind. Just go."

It was shattered. The glass. The illusions.

But perhaps it was for the best.

Because it would have ended. She had been right. All those years later, it would've ended. There would've been infidelity. There would've been messes and weeping and their children would've gone, and it would've been the two of them, not knowing how to be.

But even as she obeyed him, as she allowed herself to be driven to the private plane with her heart shattered into pieces, and her very breath painful, she foolishly wished that they'd had that life. All those years between now and heartbreak. Because at least they would've had that life.

And now, she had nothing. Nothing at all.

She knew the plane would have to stop for fuel on the East Coast, and she asked that they go through Florida.

When she ended up at her mother's new home, furnished by Rocco, her palms felt slick and sweaty.

"I need to talk to you," she said.

"What about?" her mom asked.

"Everything. I just want to know… Was everything

in my childhood a lie? Did you not love dad? Did you not love me? What did you want instead? Were you so unhappy that you were just dying to get out?"

Her mom's face softened. "Come in, Noelle."

Noelle did. The house itself was an explosion of color. Rocco would hate it, and that kind of amused her.

"Do you want a margarita?"

"No," Noelle said, feeling somewhat taken aback by the question.

"Well, I might have one. I'm surprised you're finally asking these questions."

"Well. I don't think I wanted the answers to them before."

"I think that's kind of the moral of the story, honey. It's really easy to not ask questions when you're afraid of what the answers might be."

Noelle frowned. "Do you mean you?"

Her mother got out margarita mix, tequila and ice, and poured it all into the blender. She pushed the button, and it twirled around while Noelle stood there, trying to find her equilibrium.

"That was my whole marriage to your father. Being afraid of asking questions. Afraid of what the answers would be. But no, I wasn't unhappy the whole time. And of course I loved him. I love you."

"Then why did you have an affair?"

"Because things are complicated sometimes. And I'm not perfect. Because instead of talking to your father when I felt like he was distant from me, I thought it was easier to pour my heart out to a man who didn't actually know me. A man who wouldn't bring my own frailties into the conversation. What a neat trick that is. If you bring up the problems that you're having to your husband he might tell you things you don't want to hear. I didn't want that. No, I wanted easy. So I took easy. Except, in the end of course it wasn't. Because I hurt your dad, and I didn't actually want to do that. Whether you believe me or not. But it's easy to get caught in your own made-up stories. Way too easy. Our life wasn't a lie. It wasn't nothing. It was everything to me. And within that there were failures. On both our parts. It was imperfect, and it was hard, but it was good. You were always the best part of it. So sunny and warm and you loved everything about Holiday House. I would never have asked you to leave it."

"But you did. You wanted to sell it."

She sighed and pinched the bridge of her nose. "You were an adult, and I thought maybe it would even do you some good to have some other experiences."

"Well. Now I have had them. And honestly, they just kind of hurt."

"Being an adult hurts sometimes," her mom said. "There was no way to spare you from that forever. I… Maybe it was selfish of me. I wanted to leave some of the harder parts of that life behind. And get something out of it. I've been living a different life, and it makes me feel new. I can finally escape the ways in which I disappointed your dad. The ways I disappointed myself. It isn't that it was all bad. And in the last few years, it was really good. But it's my mistakes that haunt me now that he's gone."

"Oh," Noelle said.

She didn't know what to do with all this information. It didn't solve anything, not really. It didn't magically fix what had happened between her and Rocco. But it definitely showed her childhood through a prism of fractured glass, rather than an illusory windowpane. It wasn't half so simple as perfect or not perfect. A life her mother loved, or a life she hated. It was just human frailty. It was a difficult thing to accept. But her father was gone, and she could never really have that revelation with him. That whole realization that he was just a person like she was. Trying his best, or not on a given day.

She could still have that with her mother.

"I keep wanting things to be simple," Noelle said. "Right or wrong, happy and unhappy. Perfect."

"But it isn't."

"Rocco sent me away. Because I asked him the hard question. I told him the hard thing."

Her mom closed the distance between them and put her hand on Noelle's shoulder. "Noelle, you will always be glad you did that. Because eventually, secrets come to collect. And the unspoken things come out in ways that are far more painful than if you had just talked about them."

"But I don't have him anymore."

"I'm sorry, honey. You're welcome to live a single life with me here."

"I think I'm going to go back home. Try to get back to who I was."

"Don't do that," her mother said. "That's actually what keeps you in regret. When something changes you, you have to follow that change all the way through to the end. There's no point resisting it. That's how I ended up here." She gestured around her pink and aqua kitchen.

And Noelle realized that what her mom said was true. She couldn't go back to how she was. To how things had been.

She was going to have to persist with what was new. Figure out what living with heartbreak looked like.

"I'm still going to go back," she said. "But I'll remember what you said."

"I'm sorry I didn't have some magic words for you."

"I think you gave me better than that. You gave me the truth. And I'm thankful that you're still here to give it to me."

CHAPTER SIXTEEN

EVERYTHING WAS TERRIBLE. The worst that it had ever been. He was alone. Alone, alone, and the space closed in around him like an oppressive fog. It was unbearable. Unmanageable.

He missed her. He needed her. He had failed her.

You have to get back.

No. He didn't want that. He didn't want to go back to that dark place. *But you're already there.*

That was how he found himself going out to the old house. Going through those old gates. The property was overgrown. It was awful. It was untouched, he knew. A monument to his mother's insanity. *Why did you keep it?*

That question echoed inside of him, as he took a key and turned it in the lock, opened the door for the first time in so many years. His palms were sweating, his heart beating far too fast. Why did you keep it?

If you're so ashamed of it, why did you keep this monument to it?

Because he hadn't figured out how to let it go yet. And so it stood. A monument to all they were. To his loneliness. The smell was terrible. It was also home. He hated that truth.

He walked through the dark rooms, filled with piles, filled with shame.

His heart rate quickened, and his own fear started to mount. And suddenly, he saw each and every object in the house for what it was. Fear.

It was her grasping at anything, everything.

Fear that blocked her from giving him the love that he needed. Fear that left him alone, locked in his room.

Because that was what a need for this level of control was. And for her, as chaotic as it looked, it was control.

Just like for him... For him pushing her away had been control.

Fear directly blocked love. And as he stood there, looking at all of it, at his mother's humanity, he felt something shift within him.

He saw his mother differently.

Not her failure, but simply struggles in herself that she could not figure out how to overcome, he wanted to overcome his.

A lump was in his throat, and he walked up the stairs, to his bedroom.

He reached out and turned the doorknob. It was locked.

Locked because he had locked himself in it. Locked because he never left through that door. Because he had been afraid. Afraid, afraid, afraid.

His whole life was marked by fear.

"Enough," he said to the closed door. To the little boy

that, in his mind, was still behind it. "Enough." He turned and slammed his shoulder violently against the door.

"Unlock the door," he said. "Open this door right now." He threw his body against it again, and again. And then, with one final, brutal blow, he kicked it open. And inside was nothing.

That boy wasn't there.

He was just inside of him.

It was clean. So much space around that bed.

Empty.

He was just so tired of empty space.

He kept it empty because he was scared.

He didn't want to be afraid anymore.

He wanted Noelle. He wanted the chaotic, intense feelings that she created inside of him. The feelings that he couldn't control.

But he would learn to make them better. He wouldn't lock her away.

Because he didn't want to be ruled by fear anymore. He just wanted her love.

"I love you," he said to the room.

Maybe to Noelle. Maybe to his mother.

Perhaps to the boy that had once sat in here alone. Who had wanted to be cared for more than anything in the world, but hadn't been.

But she does.

He wanted her to. He wanted her to care for him. And he didn't want to be afraid of how much he wanted it. Not anymore. He was ready to let all this go.

So that he could embrace her.

* * *

Noelle loved Christmas in Snowflake Falls. It was always hard after Christmas. When the lights were gone, and you were left with nothing but the gray persistence of January, February, March. As winter dragged on in Wyoming, far longer than in many other states.

She felt caught in that gray haze now.

She had been right about this. That home wouldn't quite feel like home, because part of her heart was somewhere else.

Part of her heart was with him.

So when she looked up, on the much less crowded streets of Snowflake Falls, and saw him standing there, in black, severe clothes, she thought she might've hallucinated him.

"Rocco?" She said his name, as if to test her own sanity, as much as anything else.

"Yes," he said.

"What are you doing here?"

"I am here because… Because I've changed. You told me that people changed when they were in love."

Her throat went tight, tears immediately stinging her eyes. "I did tell you that."

"Well, I have changed. Because I love you. But I had… Work to do. Before I could understand it. I do now. I went back to my home. And I saw it all. All of it for what it was. My mother seeking to control everything in the house, me seeking to control everything behind that door. Both of us held captive by fear. I saw that I am like her. I am. And… I am sorry. That I'm… Like that. That I have such a strong need to control everything that… I created so much space around me I didn't have room for you. And you were all I wanted. But that space was made out of fear. I just wanted to not be so afraid. But the fear was what was holding me back from love, all this time. And I don't want to be afraid anymore."

"Oh, Rocco." She wrapped her arms around his neck, not caring who saw them. She kissed him, right there in the middle of town, and she knew that there would be talk. But that was fine.

"I wanted easy. I thought my childhood was easy and perfect, and that recreating it would… Give me that same peace that I had. I talked with my mom. She made me realize we do hurt people we love sometimes, and it doesn't mean we don't love them. And… I don't need simple. But I do need you. That is what I need to be happy. It could be here…it could be in New York…"

"It will be in both places. Because this place is you."

"But you hate it," she said.

He laughed, and the sound filled her with glory.

"I do. But I love you. And so it is an easy answer to a very easy question. I don't need control over my surroundings. I need you."

"Let's go up to Holiday House," he said.

"Okay," she said.

"You think we'll get snowed in?"

"I don't think so."

"That is a shame. Because I love being snowed in with you."

EPILOGUE

Rocco grew to love Christmas at Holiday House. It was cluttered and often noisy. Noelle's mother always came to visit. Oftentimes there were guests. The rooms were small, and their children invaded their space frequently. But he had learned to love the chaos of it all. When Noelle had had their first child, he had realized he would never truly be control of anything ever again.

To say that he had let it go graciously would be an overstatement. But he had love. So what else mattered?

Christmas Eve, ten years after their first Christmas, they walked through the snowy streets of Snowflake Falls, holding hot chocolate, their four children racing about in front of them and causing mayhem.

He stopped, and looked at the Christmas tree, at all the quaint buildings.

"You know what," he said.

"What?"

"I love it here."

Noelle's eyes went wide with shock. "You do?"

"Yes. Because my family is here. And that means it is the most wonderful place on earth."

* * * * *